Minami Nanami

Lv.10

Bottom-Tier CHARACTER TOMOZAKI

Design Yuko Mucadeya + Caiko Monma (musicagographics)

Bottom-Tier
CHARACTER
TOMOZAKI

Lv.10

Yuki Yaku

Illustration by Fly

YEN ON
New York

Bottom-Tier CHARACTER TOMOZAKI Lv.10

YUKI YAKU

Cover art by Fly
Translation by Jennifer Ward

This book is a work of fiction. Names, characters, places, and incidents are the product of the author's imagination or are used fictitiously. Any resemblance to actual events, locales, or persons, living or dead, is coincidental.

JAKU CHARA TOMOZAKI-KUN LV.10
by Yuki YAKU
© 2016 Yuki YAKU
Illustration by FLY
All rights reserved.
Original Japanese edition published by SHOGAKUKAN.
English translation rights in the United States of America, Canada, the United Kingdom, Ireland, Australia, and New Zealand arranged with SHOGAKUKAN through Tuttle-Mori Agency, Inc.

English translation © 2023 by Yen Press, LLC

Yen On
150 West 30th Street, 19th Floor
New York, NY 10001

Visit us at yenpress.com
facebook.com/yenpress
twitter.com/yenpress
yenpress.tumblr.com
instagram.com/yenpress

First Yen On Edition: June 2023
Edited by Yen On Editorial: Anna Powers
Designed by Yen Press Design: Wendy Chan

Yen On is an imprint of Yen Press, LLC.
The Yen On name and logo are trademarks of Yen Press, LLC.

The publisher is not responsible for websites (or their content) that are not owned by the publisher.

Library of Congress Cataloging-in-Publication Data
Names: Yaku, Yuki, author. | Fly, 1963- illustrator. | Ward, Jennifer, translator.
Title: Bottom-tier character Tomozaki / Yuki Yaku ; illustration by Fly ; v. 1 - 8.5: translation by Winifred Bird ;
    v. 9 - 10: translation by Jennifer Ward.
Other titles: Jyakukyara Tomozaki-kun. English
Description: First Yen On edition. | New York : Yen On, 2019-
Identifiers: LCCN 2019017466 | ISBN 9781975358259 (v. 1 : pbk.) | ISBN 9781975384586 (v. 2 : pbk.) |
    ISBN 9781975384593 (v. 3 : pbk.) | ISBN 9781975384609 (v. 4 : pbk.) | ISBN 9781975384616 (v. 5 : pbk.) |
    ISBN 9781975384623 (v. 6 : pbk.) | ISBN 9781975320386 (v. 6.5 : pbk.) | ISBN 9781975333461 (v. 7 : pbk.) |
    ISBN 9781975335502 (v. 8 : pbk.) | ISBN 9781975338404 (v. 8.5 : pbk.) | ISBN 9781975338411 (v. 9 : pbk.) |
    ISBN 9781975360283 (v. 10 : pbk.)
Subjects: LCSH: Video games-Fiction. | Video gamers-Fiction.
Classification: LCC PL877.5.A35 J9313 2019 | DDC 895.63/6-dc23
LC record available at https://lccn.loc.gov/2019017466

ISBNs: 978-1-9753-6028-3 (paperback)
        978-1-9753-6437-3 (ebook)

10 9 8 7 6 5 4 3 2 1

LSC-C

Printed in the United States of America

Bottom-Tier CHARACTER TOMOZAKI

Lv.10

Characters

Fumiya Tomozaki
Second-year high school student. Bottom-tier.

Aoi Hinami
Second-year high school student. Perfect heroine of the school.

Minami Nanami
Second-year high school student. Class clown.

Hanabi Natsubayashi
Second-year high school student. Small.

Yuzu Izumi
Second-year high school student. Hot.

Fuka Kikuchi
Second-year high school student. Bookworm.

Takahiro Mizusawa
Second-year high school student. Wants to be a beautician.

Shuji Nakamura
Second-year high school student. Class boss.

Takei
Second-year high school student. Built.

Tsugumi Narita
First-year high school student. Easygoing.

Erika Konno
Second-year high school student. Queen of the class.

Rena
Twenty years old. Likes to drink.

Ashigaru-san
Pro *Atafami* player.

Common Honorifics

In order to preserve the authenticity of the Japanese setting of this book, we have chosen to retain the honorifics used in the original language to express the relationships between characters.

No honorific: Indicates familiarity or closeness; if used without permission or reason, addressing someone in this manner would constitute an insult.

-*san*: The Japanese equivalent of Mr./Mrs./Miss. If a situation calls for politeness, this is the fail-safe honorific.

-*kun*: Used most often when referring to boys, this indicates affection or familiarity. Occasionally used by older men among their peers, but it may also be used by anyone referring to a person of lower standing.

-*chan*: An affectionate honorific indicating familiarity used mostly in reference to girls; also used in reference to cute persons or animals of either gender.

-*senpai*: An honorific indicating respect for a senior member of an organization. Often used by younger students with their upperclassmen at school.

-*sensei*: An honorific indicating respect for a master of some field of study. Perhaps most commonly known as the form of address for teachers in school.

Minami Nanami ♂

The theorem that demonstrates that every system is imperfect also proves its own imperfection.

I saw myself in that line of numbers with all its contradictions.

It showed me that the truth, in the real sense, will never be found. The one thing you can believe in is that nothing's perfect. That fact might bring you despair, or maybe hope. But more than that, the ice-cold feel of it just being the truth was my style.

You can place value in clever literary expressions or will yourself to believe that every little fluctuation in your heart is the truth.

You can switch off your brain and immerse yourself in poetic sentiments to make yourself feel something powerful. Sympathy can be very pleasant.

There's nothing I dislike more than believing in something false. A story written to help you lose sight of reality, like a painkiller, is nothing more than a temporary distraction. A proof plainly indicates its substance, and that feels far kinder to me.

I can't say I'm not lonely; pretending otherwise would just be a facade. But being right matters to me more than temporary distraction, and that's my unadulterated truth.

Thinking about it now, we've been paralyzed for a long time.

Everyone else is anesthetized with comfortable lies.

While I am frozen in ice-cold logic.

Lies, and logic. It's obvious at a glance which is more attractive to people. I'd chosen isolation in order to find the truth, even if that wasn't my original intent.

Everything I'd done to argue down the world was gradually leading to a likelihood.

Like a lion tamer who subdues a beast's strength, I had gained control over that frivolity.

The results don't lie.
The results don't lie.
The results are the only thing that doesn't lie.

Someone nurtured friendships, built a relationship, experienced failure. You might sympathize with that. It might even stir your emotions.

But I don't believe in happiness based on vicarious experience.

It's gonna take more than that to save me.

1

Events that only happen on certain days are generally important

It was just me that morning in Sewing Room #2.

I'd known it would be like this before I went in. Even if she had actually been sitting there with her usual brusque expression, I wouldn't have known what to talk about. So I was relieved, in a way.

But I still wished she was there.

I had called out Hinami for the motivation behind her irrational behavior.

Basically, I'd confronted her with the reason she'd been coaching me on playing the game of life.

About two weeks had passed since Hinami had stopped coming here, and she hadn't contacted me at all.

It was mid-February. The keen sense of loss of something I'd wanted to believe in left my fingers chilled, but still, that selfish hope tightened around my heart. I knew waiting here wouldn't make her change her mind, but I was here because I didn't know when to quit. If I went to the classroom, Hinami would be there—but that wasn't the Hinami I wanted to talk to.

Nothing about this was strange, though. I should have expected it.

Hinami had just been using the character "Fumiya Tomozaki" to prove she was right. Now that I was onto her, she couldn't continue with her proof.

—*iiing dong*, —*aaang bong*.

*   *   *

The warning bell rang from the new school building, on the other side of the courtyard. The sound was clipping or something; there must have been some connection problem with the broken speakers of the old school building. Sometimes, it filled out, just in time to torture your ears again. The crackling reminded me of an old radio, and the mingled disquiet and nostalgia of the sound strangely fit my mood that moment.

I'd been notified this way that my time was up many times over the past few days.

"...Guess she's not coming."

I sighed, then picked up the bag I'd left on her usual seat, as if I'd been saving it for her. Then I started off alone down the familiar hallway.

*   *   *

While I was walking, I'd opened up my LINE chat screen with Hinami.

[*I'll be waiting in Sewing Room #2 tomorrow morning.*]

[*I'm going tomorrow, too.*]

[*I'm going to keep going down there every time, so come if you feel like it.*]

I'd sent several messages to Hinami.

I'd gotten no replies, just the "read" notifications.

I understood that continuing to message someone who's left you on read was generally seen as a social faux pas. But I still had to do it.

Aoi Hinami had been using my life.

I thought we'd shared something of a connection; maybe that was just my imagination.

But I was still fixated on her anyway, and I couldn't even put the reason for that into words.

Was it dependence? Sentimentality? Something else?
I wanted to understand.

Ashigaru-san had identified my karma.
Individualism: not overstepping with others, while keeping them from encroaching on your territory.
I was a solo competitive gamer. I instinctively rejected relationships where you entrusted responsibility for choices to someone else—or took on responsibility for another—and that instinct had taken root deep in my heart.
I didn't think I'd be able to go arm in arm with anyone, not in the real sense.

But that time, it seemed to me that I'd transgressed a boundary line—
In just one area, I'd crossed the boundaries of individualism.
I wanted to know the reason for that.

And the one thing I knew.
When I found out that she was using her own life and mine purely for the sake of proving something.

The only emotion I could feel about it was sadness.

* * *

When I entered the classroom, my eyes were naturally drawn in one direction.
"Sure, Sakura, but who are you giving your actual chocolates to?" Hinami was having a friendly chat with Mimimi, Tama-chan, and some others, and right that moment, she was in the middle of teasing Kashiwazaki-san in that same group.
"There you go avoiding the subject, Aoi!"
"It's your fault for letting me get away with it!"

A vulnerable smile, casual words. That slight intimacy in her attitude, implying her trust.

It was layer upon careful layer for the sake of charming people and maneuvering for social success.

That thoroughness was what made her Aoi Hinami, and it was why I respected her as a gamer. But the fact of the matter was that what she was doing there was far more cruel than just social maneuvering.

"That's not fair, Aoi!"

It wasn't like she was deceiving anyone. This wasn't flattery, either.

She was using other people, showing her work in her proof of correctness. That was who Aoi Hinami really was.

Kashiwazaki-san, smiling in sincere enjoyment, clearly believed in Hinami. She even seemed proud that she could talk on an equal basis with her.

Hinami was perfect, but a little clumsy, and that was exactly why everyone loved and respected her.

It was nice to be in a group with a girl like that, and it was valuable, too.

Clothing herself in a skillfully controlled shell, stimulating others' desire for acknowledgment and belonging, she hacked everything about the world. That was the design of "Aoi Hinami" that she had constructed for herself.

So during that back-and-forth between Aoi Hinami and Kashiwazaki-san, there was no connection between their hearts at all.

Mimimi must have felt my gaze; she looked over, and our eyes met. She approached, waving her arm, and smiled at me. "Morning! You're late as usual, Brain!"

Mimimi had been interacting with me more over the past few days. Was that because she knew I'd been feeling down about that thing with Kikuchi-san recently? Because she'd noticed that I'd been acting strange lately? Did she just have nothing better to do? I didn't know, but it was helpful to me.

"O-oh, am I?" I replied, trying to act normal.

Mimimi lowered her voice a little once she was in front of me. "Hey, Tomozaki. I just want to check something with you…" She said it so only I could hear, making me tense up. A while back, when I'd been thinking about slowly cutting off my relationships with everyone, Mimimi had been the first one to notice.

So had she picked up on something again? Apparently not.

"We were talking about giving out chocolates to the whole group…but is Fuka-chan okay with that sort of thing?"

"Chocolates…?" I asked, but then I immediately figured it out. "Oh. It's okay. I'm meeting her after school."

"Oh, then great!"

Yes, it was the fourteenth of February—Valentine's Day.

"I mean, I wouldn't be surprised to hear that you'd completely forgotten about something like that," Mimimi added.

"Sh-shut up. I'm actually better than I used to be."

"Ah-ha-ha, for sure!"

It was my and Kikuchi-san's first Valentine's since we'd started dating, so we'd made plans to meet after school. By the way, I'd forgotten about that until a week ago, which I do regret.

"We are dating, after all…so yeah." I was delineating where my responsibility to her lay.

Kikuchi-san and I still hadn't managed to build a relationship where we entrusted responsibility to each other. But maybe here, somewhere between zero and one hundred, we could find a place to compromise.

So even if this was what you might call another formality, we'd decided to invest this time in our relationship. Kikuchi-san respected my values in wanting the individual to live as an individual—my karma.

"Yeah…of course," Mimimi said.

I was no longer the bottom-tier character I had been before, so I think I understood what that little pause of Mimimi's meant.

But I could only carry so many things, and that implication was one of the ones I couldn't take responsibility for. Doing any more now would be overstepping.

"Aaaall righty! Then be sure to wait eagerly for your *obligatory chocolate* from me!" Mimimi flung out some dangerous terms at me with exaggerated gestures and body language.

But I was playing it safe with my reply. "…Ah-ha-ha, yeah, I'm looking forward to it." This wasn't lying, or an expression of insincerity.

I'd just decided to follow my internal priority ranking.

"Mm… Look forward to it," Mimimi replied, speaking at the same level of distance as I had.

She had already spilled out from my grasp. There was nothing for it but to stick to language I could take responsibility for.

I'd come to understand that keenly over the past few months.

And then right at that moment…

"Mimimiii, what's up?" That natural-sounding and cheery greeting came from none other than Aoi Hinami. She was looking at Mimimi and me with a dissatisfied but teasing smile. Since we'd slipped away from the others to talk, that was the natural attitude to take with us.

But…

"Heh-heh-heh! I can't tell you!"

"Hey, come on. So then…" The expression on that impenetrable mask shifted effortlessly, even though I knew her heart was buried at the bottom of a bog. "—*You* tell me, Tomozaki-kun!"

Her words were void of any honesty, sincerity, or responsibility.

The fact that Hinami would say my name like this, in the same way she always did—

This meaningless communication produced by her dark-gray logic left my heart cold.

* * *

At lunch that day, I was with the usual crowd in the cafeteria for the gifting of the chocolate. It was a big family: eight people around the large table at the back. With Nakamura, Mizusawa, Takei, and me on the boys' side, and then Hinami, Izumi, Mimimi, and Tama-chan on the girls' side, all the usual suspects were here. Everyone had already finished eating their lunches, and we were getting to the presentation of the chocolates.

Hinami was sitting in front of me and to the right, the usual perfect heroine with an affable smile on. She was just Aoi Hinami.

"All right, you bastards, take yer goods!"

The one handing out chocolate like a bandit distributing the spoils was, of course, Mimimi. As she smoothly handed me a transparent bag, I saw the star-shaped chocolates inside, with a red-and-white marble pattern on them. They looked like gnarled starfish, but I didn't really get what they were actually supposed to be. It was very apparent that they were handmade.

By the way, Mimimi was handing out chocolates to the girls as well as the boys. I guess that's what they call friend chocolate. Inclusion, I suppose.

"Huh? The hell are these?" Nakamura said flatly with a scowl. His unforgettably intimidating face had come at the cost of any sense of tact.

But Mimimi wasn't bothered by his gruffness. "Heh-heh-heh, you can't tell?" she said with a fearless grin, stroking an invisible goatee.

It wasn't just me and Nakamura who weren't getting it. Hinami was also staring at them blankly. "...Starfish?"

"Nooo!" Minami was grinning like she found this funny, but it felt a little unusual for Hinami's conclusion to be off with something like this. The fact that her wrong answer was the same as mine was even more unusual. I couldn't decide if she had guessed wrong deliberately or if she honestly didn't know, but either way, I was sure it wasn't a big deal to her.

Meanwhile, Tama-chan was examining the chocolate with a smile. "Thanks! These are those things, right? The haniwa," she said without hesitation.

"Absolutely correct!" Minami chirped. "As expected of my Tama!"

"Th-they are...?" I asked doubtfully. She had to be referring to those weird charms we'd all put on our bags. These chocolates did have five parts for a head, arms, and legs, so they technically had that in common. But when I looked around, I was surprised to find that Mizusawa and Izumi also got that these were supposed to be the charms. Izumi was encouraging Mimimi. "It must have been hard to do the stripes, huh?" She has amazing kindness reflexes.

And that led straight into Izumi sharing her own chocolate. "Here, these are mine!" She handed little bags with a catlike character on them out to everyone.

The moment Takei accepted his, he opened it up gladly. "Oooh! These look good!"

I looked at what he was holding to see moist chocolate cake.

"I tried making *gâteau au chocolat*!" Izumi said.

Oh, so that's what this is. I was learning the basics here. Accepting the cake from Izumi, I gave her a "Thanks" in return.

"Me too," said Hinami as she pulled out a paper bag with a smile. "These are supposed to be really good!" From the fancy-looking packaging, I guessed these were imported.

Izumi's eyes sparkled when she spotted the box. "Ohh! I hear those are good! I've been wanting to try some!" She leaped on them with excitement.

It was surprising that only Hinami's were store-bought when everyone else's were handmade, but well, she never wasted a moment on anything. Maybe this had been yet another carefully made choice for her.

"I love these!" Tama-chan was also responding positively. As you'd expect from someone whose parents ran a bakery, it seemed she'd had them before. Well, she'd said she was going to get serious about helping out with her family's business, so she had to know about things like this. These chocolates had a reputation.

But Hinami choosing ready-made and somewhat well-known chocolates as a present was odd. She could have wound up giving the same present as someone else. Though that hadn't happened, Hinami had allowed that possibility.

Regardless, she was handing out the chocolates to everyone. "Here, Tomozaki-kun!"

She'd refused to talk to me since our last conversation and hadn't shown up to Sewing Room #2, yet here she was saying my name like always. I'd exposed her insincerity and intentions and created a fissure in our relationship of over half a year, but now it was like that had never happened.

My name sounded empty coming from her, as if she was avoiding giving it meaning.

Not knowing how she felt as she handed me those chocolates, I reached out to accept them.

"...Ah." But my hands failed to grab the box, and it slipped out onto the table with a weak *plop*.

"S-sorry," I said. When I reached out to scoop up the chocolates, Hinami reached out at the same time, and our fingers touched.

Her fingers were freezing cold, like a bloodless machine, even though they looked like the pinnacle of perfection. Even her nails were done up prettily. The disconnect left an eerie feeling in my stomach.

Hinami picked up the chocolates first.

"Are they okay? They're not broken?" she said as she handed them over.

How was I supposed to reply to that? I answered in a monotone, eyes slightly averted. "...It's fine."

What would happen if I suddenly said something? *Why are you ignoring my LINE messages? Why won't you come to Sewing Room #2?*

Maybe I was just having weird thoughts because I was sad to have lost that. After imagining that for a minute, I quickly gave up on the idea.

It wasn't like I wanted to reject Hinami's life choices—in fact, I even respected her for them as a fellow gamer handling the game of life.

So I wanted to respect the results Hinami wanted, the results she'd gotten for herself.

"And from me, *ta-daa!*"

I was drawn out back to reality by Tama-chan's cheery voice. It had a cuteness to it now that pulled me away from that dark place. Hinami's attention was already somewhere else, and we didn't look at each other.

"Whoa!! Your chocolates are so fancy, Tama!" Mimimi oohed.

"Heh-heh-heh, my family does run a bakery, after all. So they're hand-made, of course."

"Meaning these are chocolates meant for your crush—me!"

And so the beginning to my very first lively Valentine's Day was, in a sense, the most lonely one I'd ever had.

* * *

Class was over for the day. I'd left school with Kikuchi-san, and now we were sitting side by side on a bench in a park near Kita-Asaka, the station closest to her house.

"U-um, here!" she said.

Right now, of course, was time for the bequeathing of chocolates, and Kikuchi-san was giving me a blue bag.

"Th-thanks."

Unlike the chocolate-gifting during lunch, we'd already established that this gift was the "serious" kind, which made me a little fidgety and more than a little embarrassed.

I considered Kikuchi-san to be closer to me than the others, so this time with her was especially comforting after I'd been reminded of my loss.

Thinking of it now, Kikuchi-san had always helped me like this, when I'd lost something.

"I did my best with them...," she said.

Then I realized something. "Ah..."

"Wh-what is it?"

Yeah, I didn't have to look back on my life to realize this. It was obvi-ous... "This is the first time in my life I've ever gotten actual romantic chocolates from a girl..."

"?!" Kikuchi-san shrank in on herself as she looked up at me. I'd made

the decision to build a trusting relationship between us, so I wasn't going to let myself think she was reacting this way because she thought I was creepy. She was just being shy, and I was now strong enough to remind myself of that.

"M-me too!" Kikuchi-san pushed the chocolate at my chest with both hands. "This is the first time in my life I've ever made some myself…or given serious chocolates to someone…!"

"?!"

Now what she'd said was getting to me, and I was about to react just like her. But if I made myself small, I wouldn't just be putting myself down; I'd probably look like I was cringing. So I just let my face get hot. I mean, technically, I wouldn't be able to stop my face from getting hot even if I tried.

"Um, I'm glad…," I said, "Though, I don't know if I should say that…"

"I-I'm…glad…that I could be the one to give you your first serious chocolates, Fumiya-kun…"

"O-oh." That felt meaningful, and now my face was even redder.

I dunno, it's like, talking about this myself—it was the kind of exchange that would make me want to complain, *Get a room!* But I wasn't doing it deliberately, so please cut me some slack. I was now paying the bill for all the times I'd mentally cursed the thousands of flirting couples in the world.

"…Can I open it?" I asked.

"Mm-hmm."

I opened the whitish package, which was tied up with a pale-blue ribbon. When you think Valentine's, you really tend to imagine red, pink, or hearts—it was very Kikuchi-san to choose something on the cooler spectrum instead, a pale blue. It added to that feeling that this was where I belonged, here, a little off-center. It made me feel kind of glad.

"Oh! …These look good."

Inside the package were chocolates with lots of some sort of white powder on them. A very Kikuchi-san kind of choice. There were five round chocolates in the palm-sized package. Thinking about how she'd put in the effort to make them just for me, the chocolates and this moment felt even more precious.

"Mind if I have one now?" I asked.

"S-sure." For some reason, Kikuchi-san seemed a little uneasy as she gave a little nod. When I tilted my head, she said, "Um...I'm just not sure whether they came out well..."

As she spoke, I thought, *Here goes,* and popped one in my mouth.

"Ahh!" Kikuchi-san yelped in surprise beside me.

I let the taste roll over my tongue, then sank my teeth into the soft chocolate. The liquid in the center was slightly bitter, a good contrast with the outer shell. The stuff on the outside seemed to be powdered sugar, and it blended with the bitter sauce and cocoa aroma to make for a really nice experience for my nose and mouth.

"It's really good..."

"Th-thank you..."

I'm not particularly good at flattery, so those were my real, unvarnished thoughts. And really, this chocolate was from Kikuchi-san, so that alone would make it delicious to me—I'd say there's nothing to worry about there. I'm confident that I would even wolf down a bunch of stale bread if it was from her.

Swallowing the chocolate, I retied the bag shut. "Thanks. I'll take my time eating the rest."

Should I eat it all now to let her know how much I like it...? The thought did cross my mind for a moment. But I didn't want to bolt down five on the spot and be a real glutton. Yeah, that was a good call. I opened my schoolbag to tuck away Kikuchi-san's chocolate and got to my feet.

If you're doing something just because you want to please someone else, not because you want to, that's just social maneuvering.

"I'll walk you home," I said.

"O-okay!"

Once we were on our feet, I could tell Kikuchi-san's gaze was fixed downward.

I followed her gaze to my bag. *Did she see something funny in there, when it was open just now...?* I wondered, then suddenly realized. "Um, sorry, did it bother you? ...The other chocolates, I mean."

Yeah. Right there in my bag were a number of chocolates, the ones I'd gotten from everyone during lunch break.

Once we started dating, I'd come to understand that Kikuchi-san was more anxious than I'd thought about me being friendly with my other classmates—the girls especially. But she'd also said many times that she didn't want to get in the way of me broadening my world. I'd seen her wavering between those two impulses many times.

"I-I'm sorry..." Kikuchi-san neither affirmed nor denied, just apologized. I'm sure if she was going by her feelings, she'd want to tell me her anxieties, but going by her ideals, she wanted to deny them. That contradiction was difficult to resolve, but we'd gotten far enough in our relationship that I could understand that right away.

"Sorry. Umm, I know it's okay for me to accept them, but I should've been more careful so that you wouldn't have to see them, at least." That was a compromise, still maintaining my boundaries.

After a little hesitation, Kikuchi-san looked up at me. "No... It's all right," she said, hanging her head, then slid into place beside me.

"!"

Right then, there was a soft sensation on my palm. Our body heat pressed against each other; there was no room for the calm, chill air of February to get between our hands.

"I'm the only one who can do this, right...?" she said. It was like a magic spell.

"...Yeah. It's just you." I nodded, squeezing her hand back.

Even if your situation hasn't changed, just seeing it from a new angle can completely change your perspective on the world.

Kikuchi-san had taught me this very important thing—she and one other.

I'm sure this magic is needed in order to make a relationship, the way you are, "special."

I mean, this was enough to make me feel so fulfilled, and probably Kikuchi-san, too.

"…!"

But what rose in my mind then was Hinami's expression that day, and her cold fingers.

She used her own life to try to prove she was right—but that wasn't enough for her. She'd stuck her controller into a new port and changed her character to me instead. She'd even tried to prove her logic made for reproducible results.

But then she still wore that thick, cold mask of hers, adding the logic of her social maneuvering into her proof.

So when you got down to it, her emptiness, that something she'd lost—

—it meant that she'd been unable to fulfill herself with the proof that used the both of us.

She had the position she wanted in the class; she was respected by everyone and well-liked. She'd changed my appearance, the way I talked, even the way I dealt with people—everything. She'd even had me make the ideal girlfriend in Kikuchi-san, someone who truly understood me.

If Hinami still didn't feel fulfilled—what else would she have to achieve to actualize what she thought was correct?

"…Tomozaki-kun, what's wrong?" Kikuchi-san asked me.

"Oh, no… It's nothing."

With feelings that we couldn't talk about still lingering, but still clearly holding hands, Kikuchi-san and I started walking back home.

* * *

When we approached the usual bridge, Kikuchi-san slowed down and asked me, "Were things…all right after that?"

Though I'd half guessed what she meant, I had the sense that she was scared to actually talk about it. "After what?" I asked.

"Um…I was wondering if something happened with Hinami-san…"

Kikuchi-san had heard bits of the story from me, and she also had her insight in her stories about Alucia. Kikuchi-san had gotten very close to the core of Hinami's motivations with relatively little to go on.

She'd given me some major hints that had enabled me to realize the truth, but at the same time, it was as if I'd reached down and dredged something up out of the darkness, and now I couldn't put it back.

That was why I hesitated. "…Umm."

The intentions behind Hinami's actions, which I'd confronted her with, were very grotesque in a sense, but in another sense, it was also so incredibly earnest of her.

She really was just like the bloodless girl Alucia from *Pureblood Hybrid and Ice Cream*, pursuing commonly accepted values for the sake of self-affirmation.

It was that exact same solitary struggle, that hungering for a foundation for one's own existence.

"It's just like you said, Kikuchi-san."

I thought that this was the one thing I should say.

"Hinami was…Alucia."

That would be enough for her to basically understand. The parts that she couldn't understand were because they were private to Aoi Hinami, and there was no need for her to know everything. That's what I thought.

"…I see." Kikuchi-san's gaze lowered, and she bit her lip. "So then Hinami-san has still been fighting the whole time…"

"*Fighting*… Yeah, you're right."

That word felt oddly right in describing Hinami.

Saying things she didn't believe, treating her relationships with others like tools, making it seem to other people like their hearts were connected when they weren't at all—

You'd think all that could come of this was irreparable isolation, but she somehow picked out her perfectly correct logic and leaned on that instead.

If that's not a fight, then what is?

"She's been…fighting all today, too," I said.

We both knew the story. We knew Alucia.

"On the Wings of the Unknown."

"Pureblood Hybrid and Ice Cream."

Though Alucia, as she appeared in these two stories, differed in her birth and upbringing, the way that she didn't have anything she wanted to do and guaranteed her value just by acquiring what society thought was valuable was the same.

Alucia was talented, intelligent, and beautiful.

But she suffered, struggled, and continued to fight because she had nothing like a core that she could truly love. She had no blood that would decide her race or who to be.

She was always…alone.

"Um…Fumiya-kun."

"…Yeah?"

And there was one more story that Kikuchi-san and I shared.

"Is Hinami-san still teaching you how to play the game of life?"

That was the game of life, by Hinami and me.

"…I'm not sure."

I couldn't answer that question.

I'd been sure there was meaning behind everything Hinami did. But Hinami had kept on coaching me in life strategy—something that didn't benefit her at all, at first glance. Kikuchi-san had questioned me about that contradiction, and after I'd figured out the truth, I'd told Hinami about it and checked my answers with her.

And then I hadn't managed to speak with her since—not even once.

"Maybe it's over," I said.

Kikuchi-san went pale. "…Huh? Wh-why…? The relationship was important to you, wasn't it?"

"…Yeah, but…"

"I'm sorry, it's because I butted in—"

"No, it's not that." I kept her from blaming herself. But this wasn't just me trying to be nice. "I would have had to find out about that eventually." I'd wanted it, too.

I'd always wondered it.

"If I was going to continue our relationship, I would have had to… overstep eventually."

I'd thought of myself as an individualist.

But with Hinami—only Hinami—I wanted to step over the line.

That wasn't because Kikuchi-san had told me to. It was a feeling that had always been drifting around in my heart.

"You want to…change Hinami-san's world, huh," she said. Her voice sounded sorrowful somehow. I'd told Kikuchi-san about that wish I had in Sewing Room #2.

With Kikuchi-san, I still hadn't managed to overcome this wall I had. I was still on the way there, aiming for a relationship in the future where we could entrust each other with responsibility.

But Kikuchi-san knew that Hinami-san and I didn't have that.

"…Yeah… But…" With Kikuchi-san's direct gaze questioning me, I thought back one more time on Hinami's real motivations.

Then I recalled the conversation with her I'd had a few days ago.

"Is that really what I want to do…?" I was unsure now.

"…Do you mean…?" Kikuchi-san trailed off.

I really didn't know anymore.

"I told her what I thought…and then Hinami didn't deny it. She gave me a sad look, like, *Of course you're angry*, and left the room." That had happened two weeks ago now, but the cold, lonely sound of her voice lingered vividly in my ears. "When I send her messages on LINE, I get no answer, and when we're with everyone, Hinami treats me like nothing happened…"

Maybe what really made me sad was that—

*　　*　　*

"Right now, I'm being rejected."

Maybe that was a strong way to put it. But it really felt like that.

"Oh…" Kikuchi-san watched me with dewy eyes.

It brought back the events of that summer.

Thinking about it now, Hinami had rejected me then, too.

Then Kikuchi-san had given me the courage to go see Hinami one more time.

"Sorry for complaining again…," I said. "I'll think a little more about it and try coming up with an answer."

I couldn't make her shoulder that again—and she was my girlfriend now. I would choose to deal with this problem myself.

"…I understand." Kikuchi-san seemed sorrowful and somehow resigned as she nodded. "No matter what you do—I'll support you."

"Yeah…thanks."

And so having told her everything I had to, I was holding her hand.

I couldn't deny Aoi Hinami was special to me, but—

—the one who I liked as a girl, as my girlfriend, and the one I wanted to spend the most time with, was Kikuchi-san.

Right after we made that confirmation with each other, unexpected news came to me.

*　*　*

"Hinami's birthday?"

It was the next day, after school.

Seven of us from the chocolate gifting the other day had gotten together—it was minus Hinami—and now Mimimi had some surprising info.

"Yep, yep! We're having a party!" she said.

"Heck yeah!" Takei crowed as they both thrust up fists, and everyone nodded along.

Apparently, March 19 was Hinami's birthday, and everyone was excited to celebrate it. By the way, the girl in question had been nabbed by the student council today, so we were using that opportunity to discuss.

"So Hinami's birthday is next month?" I said.

"Uh-huh. Wait, does that mean you didn't know, Fumiya? That's pretty surprising." Mizusawa seemed like he meant a lot by that, making me wince a little.

"Is it...?"

I've never had any kind of talk with Hinami about her birthday, for starters. And even if we had known each other's birthdays and they were celebrated at school on those days as a formality, we didn't have the kind of relationship where we'd send personal messages to each other.

"Umm." I wasn't sure how to answer, but I decided to speak frankly. "I don't know, and I don't think Hinami knows my birthday, either..."

Izumi's eyes widened in surprise. "Huh! I thought Aoi would celebrate the birthdays of just about everyone in class!"

"Come on, what are you imagining here...? Wait, I guess I can't say that when it comes to Hinami..."

"Ah-ha-ha! Right?!"

People found it surprising that Aoi Hinami hadn't celebrated the birthday of a classmate. Most people wouldn't call that normal. If you didn't know more about her, you'd think, *She's such an earnest person*, or if you were going to probe deeper, at most, you'd imagine, *She's trying real hard to be liked.*

If they found out that every single one of those things was part of a proof, how would they all feel about the time they'd spent together?

"And thusly, there is something I, Minami Nanami, would like to do!"

"What's that?" I asked her.

Mimimi declared in a bouncy tone:

"Drumroll please—it's a surprise party!"

* * *

"Oh-ho…"

A surprise party. The term was so powerfully associated with the cool kids, it gave me mild vertigo. It also immediately had me imagining possibilities.

Izumi's eyes shone. "That's a really good idea! So then, like! I have a suggestion, too!"

"What?" Mimimi asked.

"Why don't we all go together on an overnight trip?!"

"Ohh!"

"That's an awesome idea!" Takei was all in on a fun-sounding idea. He'd immediately react to terms like *overnight*, *Salisbury steak*, and *rhinoceros beetle*, so winning him over was always simple.

But our resident realist Mizusawa was less enthusiastic. "I understand the feeling…but it's less than a year now until entrance exams, right? Do we have the time to be doing stuff like that?"

"Urk, well, you have a point…" Izumi cringed.

It was true we were in the third semester of second year. The class and teachers were all fully in gear for entrance exams.

"That was why we went camping during summer break. We had that celebration then because it would be tough to do later."

Izumi wilted, but after a few seconds, she slowly lifted her chin. "But, like…I haven't managed to repay everyone?"

"Repay everyone?" Mizusawa repeated.

Izumi nodded. "We had a lot of fun camping this summer, right? But the most fun thing about it was how everyone came up with that plan for us…" Her words were so pure, without any affectation, gradually warming the mood. Nakamura was nodding as well, though he seemed a little less enthusiastic about it.

"You guys did so much for us back then, you know! So I've been wanting to do something to make someone else happy…," she pressed.

"Well, when you put it like that…" Mizusawa started to seem hesitant. You could call this behavior "manipulation of the mood" in a way. The amazing thing about Izumi was she could do it naturally. She didn't plan out her every social move; she lived as a character, moving people with her sincere thoughts and emotions—totally opposite from Hinami.

By the way, Tama-chan didn't seem even slightly bothered by the conversation, even though she hadn't been part of the camping trip. She's got a strong core.

Then Nakamura declared, "Well…why not? A day or two seems fine." His tone was strong, although he wasn't necessarily looking at anyone. "Everyone here has some kind of a debt to her, right?" Though he was just stating his opinion, his words exerted a pressure that seemed to say, *No objections, I take it?*

So strong.

And nobody present actually had any objections.

"Ha-ha-ha, yeah, maybe you're right," Mizusawa said. He seemed to be putting up a white flag, but I wasn't sure he wanted to keep resisting.

"Yeah. I agree." Tama-chan hadn't spoken much before, but at times like this, she'll take the initiative and express her opinion directly. It was very Tama-chan of her.

As the group was starting to come into agreement, Mimimi said something unexpected. "Yeah, for sure! Like, Aoi's seemed down lately, so I'd like to hit her with some encouragement!"

"Huh?" Her remark surprised me.

And that wasn't all.

"Oh, I thought so, too! She seems a little tired, huh. Maybe she's been busy lately?" said Izumi, nodding.

"Yeah. Well, I'm sure she has a lot going on." Mizusawa indicated his agreement in turn.

"…Hinami…seems down?" I repeated. Not that it didn't make sense.

Actually, I'd also thought Hinami had seemed a little strange lately— like how she hadn't noticed that Mimimi's chocolates were haniwa, or how she gave store-bought chocolate instead of handmade. I'd also managed to ping that.

But I'd assumed that was because of what had happened between us, because the way I saw her had changed. Just overthinking.

But others had noticed it, too.

"Haven't you noticed, Brain?! She's kind of had her head in the clouds, and she doesn't seem as sharp..."

"Yeah, I get that. Like just the other day..." And then one after another, everyone started talking about Hinami's recent behavior. Including things I hadn't even thought about. I was paying close attention.

This weirdness that everyone had noticed probably wasn't something that Hinami was deliberately showing them.

I was sure it was real. She was revealing herself from underneath her mask.

"She doesn't really talk to us about stuff like that," said Mizusawa.

"We want her to rely on us more, right?!" said Izumi.

I wonder why—that fact felt so overwhelming to me.

"If we're going to do something for Aoi to repay her, then her birthday is it!" Mimimi was nodding, too.

"Okay then! How about we all choose a present for her?" Izumi said excitedly.

Mizusawa nodded, his eyes bright. "I like that idea. But I dunno about all of us just choosing one thing. Seems kinda sad."

One after another, ideas on how to please Hinami started flying back and forth.

"One present each from all of us would be too much," said Nakamura.

"So then how about getting a total of three?" Tama-chan suggested. She and Nakamura hadn't gotten along well before, but now even they were engaging with each other toward the same goal. They all wanted to cheer Hinami up and show how much they cared.

That was when a light bulb lit over Mimimi's head with a *ding*. "Okay! So then how about we split into three teams to come up with surprises?!"

Mizusawa immediately nodded. "Oh, that might be a good idea. Like a competition."

"A competition?! Hell yeah!!" Takei piped up as well. It was in his nature to automatically react to words like *competition, curry bread,* and *free extra-large.*

"I like that idea! You mean like, which team makes Aoi happiest, right?!" Izumi's voice was innocently bouncy.

Then Mizusawa smiled with an "I see" as he summed up the whole discussion into one remark:

"Okay—so this is the Make Hinami Happy Championship."

"Yeah!"

Everyone started chattering excitedly about that title.

Watching them, I was stunned.

Maybe I'd been thinking too hard.

When I'd learned how Hinami really felt, I'd started to feel doubt, unease, and sadness about how she used her relationships with others, how all she could do was follow her proof with herself. I'd kept wondering how she'd wound up like that and how I could make her stop.

But all everyone was thinking now was *What would make Aoi Hinami happy?*

That was it.

"…Ha-ha." A laugh slipped out of me, and before I knew it, I was swept up in the mood around me. "Yeah, that's right." Suddenly, I was nodding along.

Aoi Hinami had said that the mood was the absolute worst norm, established in the moment.

Speaking in terms of that definition, maybe I was just letting everyone else affect me right now. —But.

"Let's do it. A birthday party to make Hinami happy," I said to everyone, putting a stamp on it at the end.

They could all sense I was being a bit overly emphatic about this, so I was getting some dubious looks.

I used the skills I had gained from Hinami, controlling my facial expression and tone of voice. "I want to make her happy," I declared with confidence.

Of course, these were Hinami's friends, and they didn't know her true motives. Really, it was obvious they would be taking this approach.

But that simple goodwill—that simple honesty that plunged onward regardless of the truth—maybe that was important in considering her feelings.

I'd forgotten that.

I don't know if my expression was strange, or maybe Mizusawa's intuition was just that sharp, but he lowered his voice and said, "What's wrong, Fumiya?"

I turned to him. "...I was just thinking that like...maybe I wasn't being as considerate of Hinami as I thought."

"Hmm," Mizusawa said with a raised eyebrow. Then he smiled, letting his true intent show through. "Well, when you care about something, you can't stay cool about it," he told me. That expression of his made him seem reliable, but also grating. For some reason, he seemed kind of different from usual. More aggressive.

One of the things I wanted to do was teach Aoi Hinami the enjoyment to be found in life.

So rather than trying to learn what was behind her mask, rather than trying to expose her—

First—I would try to take seriously the idea of making her happy.

That might be my clue to resolving the uncertainty I was feeling right now.

"Oooookay! So then we're gonna make Aoi smile!" Mimimi said as she pumped up a fist, and the rest of us did the same.

2

When another party member specializes in an opposing element, you might get a powerful new move

It was break time, the next day.

While we were in the classroom, preparing for the next class, Hinami was chatting with Kashiwazaki-san and the others. Meanwhile, Izumi was watching her like a hawk, while the six of us watched Izumi.

"Aoiii!" Izumi hid her tension fairly well as she went over to Hinami, and we pretended to chat as we sent good vibes her way.

The first major condition for making Aoi Hinami's birthday party a success was taking Aoi on an overnight trip. But as Mizusawa had said, the time of year being what it was right now, exams were close. Well, this was Hinami with her mask on, so I'm sure she wouldn't just flatly shoot us down, but it was quite possible she might suggest alternate plans as a gentle no.

When we'd started discussing who should be the one to invite Hinami, we were initially thinking we should get Mizusawa as the one with the knack for something like this. But with Hinami particularly—

"Ahh, Mizusawa's kinda sketchy; I feel like it'd backfire on him. Shouldn't Izumi invite her instead?"
"Huh. You're so forthright these days, Fumiya."

Plus, pure and innocent Izumi was motivated to repay a debt, and so it was decided. Right now, she was clearly nervous as she tried to talk Hinami into it.

"—So that's what we were thinking. How about it?!"

By the way, since the timing was so obvious (the invitation being on the day of her birthday), we weren't going to hide that we were planning a birthday celebration. But we were keeping it secret what the celebration would be, and that we were splitting into three teams that were scheming to make her happy—the strategy was all about the content of the event.

"Umm......" To no one's surprise, Hinami looked like she was going to decline. By the way, we were in the corner of the classroom pretending to chat while glancing over at the two of them, and Hinami was definitely onto us. "I don't want to take up everyone's time now..." Hinami refused, though I don't know if that was actually her reason.

But of course, Izumi would not back down. "We want to celebrate it for you! So please!" She put her hands together and bowed her head.

But Hinami balked. "Why are you saying please to me...?"

It was a bit of a strange situation for the one throwing the party to be bowing in an effort to get the birthday girl to cooperate, but that was just Izumi. Logic didn't work on her, after all.

"You're always helping me out, so—" Izumi's words were so pure, and it was also an emotional argument. Hinami was armed with logic, but her refusal didn't mean much to Izumi.

"Urk..."

And so after some back-and-forth—

"F-fine! If you're going to insist, I'll let you throw me a party! ...Wait, what did I just say?" Hinami added in a silly tone.

"Yaaay, thanks! Hope you're looking forward to it! Oh, I'll message you to let you know about where we're going and stuff, but the details of the plan are a secret! We wanna surprise ya!" she said with a wink and lots of playfulness.

If you tell her it's a surprise, then won't it not be a surprise anymore...? I wondered, but never mind the details. Anyway, we'd succeeded in inviting Hinami, so Izumi had won, against all odds.

Izumi rushed over to us, where we welcomed her and told her she did great, which Hinami watched with an exasperated smile.

She was like a parent watching their child wreaking some sort of havoc.

I'm sure even that vulnerable expression was just another part of her proof, but for now, that was fine.

If this trip could draw out her real smile from behind the mask, it would be enough.

* * *

So everyone going on the trip aside from Hinami got together at a family restaurant after school. We'd openly told Hinami not to come because we were working on the surprise. Everything seemed on track.

"Aaall right! So we're splitting into these teams!" Mimimi said, showing us the list she'd written in her notebook in pen. For some reason, she'd doodled some weird mascot character all over it, but the layout was very readable—I should've expected as much from Mimimi after her experience with the elections. She'd transformed so much since she'd made her campaign promises.

It was a competition to please Hinami, with us split into three teams. The teams were innocuous: the usual pair of Mimimi and Tama-chan, the couple pair of Nakamura and Izumi, and the friendly pair of me and Mizusawa. And that was that.

"Yeah, I think that'll work!" Tama-chan nodded.

"Wait, wait! What about me?!" Takei cried.

"Oh, I forgot about you."

"That's so mean!"

Finally, even Tama-chan, who was the newbie to the group, was starting to tease Takei. *Don't worry about it, Takei. It's okay to go hard on him, Tama-chan.*

Takei's smile was getting all blushy as Tama-chan teased him. "…Heh-heh."

Hold on there. Oh yeah, Takei said before Tama-chan is his type. I take it back—run for your life, Tama-chan.

"Umm, then…is there a team you want to join, Takei?" I tried to tentatively confirm with him.

Takei just went straight for what he wanted. "I'd like to join Tama's group!"

"Okay, so Takei's in our group," I said.

"Huhh?!"

And so I protected Tama-chan from Takei's clutches, and Mimimi gave me a thumbs-up. *I see, it seems our interests are aligned as members of the Protect Tama-chan Committee.*

"That's all good, Fumiya, but is it okay to leave Kikuchi-san behind?" Mizusawa asked.

"Ahh…" I trailed off. I'd actually been a little worried about that. "She probably will worry…"

I'd talked with Kikuchi-san, and we'd decided that neither of us would restrict each other's behavior. Kikuchi-san had said she wanted me to be Poppol, and it was also important to me to be Poppol—someone who changes and expands their world.

But just seeing my Valentine's chocolate had been enough to make Kikuchi-san uneasy. It would be hard for her to watch her boyfriend go on an overnight trip in mixed company, even if it was a group trip.

Especially when Hinami would be there, too.

"I understand the desire to invite her if she wants to come, but…" I trailed off.

"But what?" Mimimi prompted me to continue.

Hesitating just a little, I imagined myself being with Kikuchi-san on the trip. "Wouldn't it be weird for everyone to have a couple joining in on an event like this…?"

As soon as I asked it, I felt someone shift across from me. I looked over to see Izumi's face fall. *…Oh.*

"You thought of it that way, Tomozaki...?" Izumi's gaze flicked over to Nakamura, and she looked really apologetic.

Crap, I messed that up. "N-no! That's not what I mean! Look, Kikuchi-san isn't normally a part of this group, so it's like, uh..."

"...Mm."

"That's not something I'm typically thinking about you guys, honestly!" I tried to explain myself, but I was so muddled now that everything I said was making it worse.

"It wouldn't really bother us, either," Nakamura declared in a low voice. "If Kikuchi-san says she wants to come, I don't mind. It'd be worse if you two break up over this or something."

"Nakamura..." His suggestion was brusque, but kind of considerate. Actually, I feel like he's chilled out a little since starting to date Izumi. Love changes you, I guess.

"Also, Kikuchi's been friendly with Yuzu lately, right?"

"Mm, that's right!" Izumi agreed.

It seemed that they'd kept in touch ever since they ran into each other at the shrine at New Year's. At the very least, Izumi immediately calling me that time Kikuchi-san ran out of the classroom meant that they'd built enough trust in their relationship to share important things like that.

"So it'll work out," said Nakamura. "You don't have to worry about the group or whatever." He was either trying to be considerate of me, or maybe he just trusted Izumi.

Either way, it was kinda sweet. "...Oh."

Meanwhile, Mimimi's eyes were watering up dramatically as she watched. "Wahhh! What beautiful friendship between men! I, Minami Nanami, am moved indeed!"

"This isn't friendship or anything," Nakamura shot back.

"Ooh, the aloof act just makes it better!"

"What?"

Mimimi was the same as ever, even with Nakamura, but eventually, she gathered herself and smiled at me. "But I agree with Nakamoo! Try inviting Kikuchi-san. Having more cute girls is totally welcome, actually!" She grinned wide, but eventually, it calmed a little. "Besides, I want you guys to stay together for a long time, too."

Those words reflected Mimimi's strength—and maybe weakness, too. That was why, again, I had no choice but to play it safe. "…Okay."

"With all she did for me during the play, I've been wanting to actually talk to her!" said Tama-chan, one of our lead actresses.

"Like Shuji said, we talked about love and lots of things and made friends, so we'll be okay!" Izumi added as she nodded along.

I will not think about what exactly they talked about.

"Yeah, I wanna be friends with her!" Takei declared for no reason. He was talking out of pure emotion, which was actually more reassuring than anything.

"…Thanks, guys, I'll try inviting her," I said, and everyone smiled in relief.

Suddenly, Mizusawa seemed to have just realized something. "Oh. But if Fuka-chan comes, the team's gonna be me, Fumiya, and Takei… The numbers get weird."

Now that he said it, I realized it, too. If you added Kikuchi-san to the current teams, our team would be the only one with four people.

"True," Nakamura remarked, and Mizusawa grinned.

"—So then Takei's gotta be on your team, after all, Shuji."

"Huh. Maybe I don't want Kikuchi coming after all."

"Shuji?! That's so mean!"

As Takei lamented at my periphery, our plans were firming up.

* * *

That night, in my room, I was video-chatting with Kikuchi-san.

"—So that's what we were talking about…but what do you think?"

When I told her about what the group had discussed, her gaze wavered. "But…should I go…?" she said anxiously.

I nodded at her. "Everyone was saying it's okay for you to come. They want to be friends with you." As I waited for her reply, I started rethinking how I'd accidentally passed along Takei's opinion.

But Kikuchi-san's expression remained glum. "...Oh, you think?" Seeing her reaction, I was hesitant. It didn't look like she was simply trying to be polite. Maybe Kikuchi-san didn't really want to go.

"Um, I'm not trying to force you," I said. "It's just that if you do want to come, we'd be happy to have you."

"Mm. Thank you."

And then thinking back on the story Kikuchi-san had written, I said, "Especially...if this isn't quite your fireling lake. That's fine."

Kikuchi-san paused a little when I used our shared metaphor. "Um... so then you guys don't mind if I bother you?"

That really cheered me up to hear. "Then you'll come?! I'll tell everyone!"

"Mm-hmm."

But something did bother me a little. The way things were going, I couldn't be sure I hadn't forced her. "If you ever get nervous, then you can tell me any time," I added.

Kikuchi-san gazed at her palms as if checking how she felt. "Yes... It's true, I am a little scared." Then she fixed her eyes forward. "But I've wanted to try a little adventure, too."

"...Adventure?" I repeated.

"Umm." Kikuchi-san smiled shyly. "I don't want to become friends with just anyone...but it's your friends." She trusted me. Then she giggled, and her face relaxed. "They're trying to make someone happy. They can't be bad."

"Ah-ha-ha. Yeah, I agree."

Kikuchi-san smiled, and then her expression turned a little more serious. "It's for Hinami-san, isn't it?"

I could tell those words meant a number of things, but... "...Yeah, that's right." I answered briefly and honestly.

Kikuchi-san gave me a little nod and sighed. "I've been having some regrets, just a few. I think I overstepped with Hinami-san in making the play and the novel. I want to apologize to her and make up for it. But maybe I'm just trying to feel less guilty…" I could almost see the wheels of her imagination turning as she said, "I was thinking that next time…I'd like to use Alucia for something that would make Hinami-san happy."

Her conclusion resembled the one I'd reached myself after hearing everyone talk.

"Yeah, I want to do that, too." I nodded, facing straight ahead.

Both of us were working toward the same goal as a couple—although this was about Aoi Hinami, the other person who was important to me. But I felt like this time spent sharing a goal and trying to move forward would be part of what made our relationship special.

"Then I'm counting on your help, Fumiya-kun."

And so I was joined by a very encouraging ally in the Make Hinami Happy Championship.

* * *

"H-hello!"

A few days later, we had a day off from school. I'd come to Omiya with Kikuchi-san.

But right now, it wasn't me Kikuchi-san was saying hello to.

"I-I'm glad to see you!" she said.

Waiting in front of the beanstalk statue was Mizusawa. When we got there, his eyebrows rose as he greeted us, and he gave Kikuchi-san a smile. "Yeah, likewise."

Yep—Kikuchi-san was joining the Tomozaki-Mizusawa team for the Happy Hinami Championship, that day we'd come to meet and discuss.

"I think the last time we actually talked… Was it that time with Tama?" said Mizusawa.

When Tama-chan had been trial-and-erroring her way back into the good graces of our class, we'd gotten lots of help from both Mizusawa and Kikuchi-san.

"Th-thank you for your help then!" Kikuchi-san threw herself into a deep bow. She was trying so hard not to seem rude.

"Ha-ha-ha! Hey, relax. *You're* not gonna get grabbed and eaten," Mizusawa said, easygoing and making frivolous remarks as always.

"So you're eating someone else? Dude," I shot back at him as I came up at his side, along with Kikuchi-san.

"Umm, so then are we going to go to some café?" I made a hopefully safe suggestion.

Agreeing with me, Mizusawa said, "Oh, then hey, there's someplace I'd like to go, you mind?"

"Hmm? Oh, okay."

Then Mizusawa got a mysteriously smirky kind of look. Well, it should be fine to leave these things to Mizusawa.

—Or so I thought. Before long, I wanted to pull my hair out.

* * *

"Welco... Wait, Tomozaki-san and Mizusawa-san?!"

The elevator opened up to reveal the shop to the three of us. That cry of surprise had come from Gumi-chan, who was standing at the register.

Yup—after saying there was someplace he wanted to go, Mizusawa had taken us to Karaoke Sevens, where he and I worked.

"C'mon, Mizusawa, what is this about?" I demanded.

"Yeah, Mizusawa-san! What's going on?!" Gumi-chan chimed in.

"Uh, I don't know why you're acting like that, too, Gumi-chan."

"Oh, was I too obvious? I was just going along with you," Gumi-chan said carelessly in her usual lazy manner. Looking closely, she was leaning her body weight on the wall in a way that you just barely couldn't tell— she was such a master-level slacker.

Watching Gumi-chan, Mizusawa whispered conspiratorially in my ear, "So it's about time for you to introduce your girlfriend now, right?"

"?!"

And then he was suddenly walking up to the register counter. "Can we use a room? Also, we're hoping for a discount on the food."

"Sure, but just the fried stuff! The rice bowls take more man-hours, so none of those."

"Yeah, fine, fine." The two of them chatted as they went through the front-desk registration.

Well, I saw the same stuff all the time at work, but Mizusawa's scheming had left me way too worked up for this.

I couldn't stay out of this forever, though, so I walked up to the register, "Umm...hi, Gumi-chan."

Meanwhile, Kikuchi-san popped her face out from behind me. "H-hello..."

"Hello... Wait, it's a super-cute girl?!" Gumi-chan was surprised, bringing her weight off the wall to lean out over the register in a flowing kind of motion. Prowess expected of a master in the art.

"Whose?! Whose girl is she?!"

"Hey..."

"Ah...no way! Don't say she's with both?!" Gumi-chan blurted out with the grace of a jackhammer.

"Don't say messed up stuff." Mizusawa gave her a jab in return.

But Gumi-chan is a mollusk; she absorbs physical damage. She'd be a great late-game boss.

Mizusawa just looked over to me and said, "—She's asking whose girl she is." He gave me a rather chipper smirk. He can really be like this sometimes. He was totally screwing with me.

"Ah..." I looked over to Kikuchi-san for help.

"...!"

But surprisingly, she seemed to be looking forward to me introducing her.

Oh yeah, Kikuchi-san can be like this sometimes. These two combined are gonna be a lot of trouble.

"So what is it, Tomozaki-kun?! Hurry, while I can stay on my feet!"

That was a pretty ridiculous condition for her demand. But it was true that she wasn't leaning her weight on anything. This was rare. I was curious about what would happen if I failed to say it while she could stay standing up straight, but well, there was no reason not to say it.

All right, then—just yolo it.

"Umm, this is Kikuchi-san…my girlfriend."

"…!"

The moment I said it, Kikuchi-san's face burst into red as if she'd been bracing herself—she really can be like that sometimes. Well, it was cute in a way, but now Gumi-chan eyeing us coolly, like *Look at them flirt…* This was so uncomfortable. Gumi-chan won't try to hide those thoughts in any way.

"So you turn into one of those shy and bashful guys when you get a girlfriend, huh…? Just how much do you love her…?"

"H-hey, it's not like—" I just about got pulled into denying it, but once again, I felt a gaze from the side. I turned my head over that way to see Kikuchi-san's face fall a little bit.

"W-wait, no! Um…yes, that is true… I love her a lot…"

"…!"

"Look! I knew it!"

"Ha-ha-ha! You said it, Fumiya."

And so with absolutely no one on my side, I was overwhelmed.

* * *

"Then enjoy."

It had been about ten minutes since we'd all poured ourselves drinks at the drink bar and settled into the largish room at Karaoke Sevens.

When the free combo from Gumi-chan arrived, Mizusawa got us started. "All right. What sort of surprise should we do?"

"Yeah…where do we start?" I said, tossing the conversation toward Kikuchi-san.

She thought for a moment. "Hmm…the most important thing really has to be…what Hinami-san likes, right?"

"Umm, well, for Hinami…then cheese," I said, as a place to start.

Mizusawa nodded. "Well, if you want to be as predictable as possible." "I'm sure part of that is her deliberately exaggerating it, but she does legit like cheese."

"Huhh, so you see it that way, too." Mizusawa seemed to be trying to get something out of me as he laid his chin on the back of his hand.

"Wh-what do you mean, I 'see it that way'?"

"Oh, nothing. Go on, go on." He was studying my expression while Kikuchi-san watched us curiously.

"Umm, and then…" Then the first thing that came to mind was what had brought Hinami and me together in the first place: the game that was the one arena where I could beat her. It was *Atafami*.

—But.

"Also…oh yeah, track!" I offered the safe answer.

That competitive arena was connected to Hinami's secret of liking *Atafami*, though not directly, so I unconsciously avoided referring to it.

"Track, huh." Mizusawa leaned his weight on the table. He was laying on the pressure now; he knew that was a weak answer. His gaze was piercing.

"U-um…and also…like, um…" He hadn't said anything, but I felt like he was cross-examining me. Kikuchi-san was watching us with even deeper curiosity than before.

"…Well, true, I guess that's it," said Mizusawa.

"Th-that's it…?"

Eventually, he sighed and leaned back onto the sofa again. But his eyes never left me as he continued, "…Listen. There's something I want to say to you, and to Fuka-chan."

"Y-yes?" Kikuchi-san was startled to hear her name called.

Mizusawa sank into the synthetic leather sofa and commented, "So I have a crush on Aoi."

Both me and Kikuchi-san yelped. "Huh?!" "Wha?!"

I already knew, but the timing and small-talk delivery of the information caught me off guard. I was just as surprised as Kikuchi-san. Mizusawa smiled, and I could tell he'd been gunning for that reaction. You really have to watch out with this guy.

"H-hey, where's this coming from?" I asked.

"You knew about this already, right, Fumiya?"

"It's still surprising to hear it out of the blue!"

"Ha-ha-ha, sorry, sorry." With his detached expression, you really couldn't tell what he was thinking. "But this is important," he said calmly, before a bit of heat entered his voice.

"This time...I'm not fooling around. I seriously want to make Aoi happy."

Normally, Mizusawa came off like such a sketchy womanizer, but his eyes right now were dead serious. Kikuchi-san could sense it, too.

"...I see." Kikuchi-san smiled kindly.

"So I don't want this surprise to just be a formality. Let's do something for her that will touch her heart," he said with determination.

"Formality...huh," I echoed.

Mizusawa had told me about that way of thinking before.

That was when you prioritized the way something looked or sounded, its social image, to compensate for the content.

Mizusawa had been trying to do away with that for a while now.

"...Yeah, fair enough." I was nodding, too. Hinami didn't show us in the way she communicated with us what she really thought or who she really was—she was always just going through the motions. So Izumi and Mimimi and the others would only have seen what was on the surface.

But I thought I knew a thing or two about what was beneath her mask.

"Since we're doing this, you wanna make it the greatest birthday party ever, right?" Mizusawa said with a kind grin.

"...This is a little surprising," said Kikuchi-san, watching Mizusawa.

"What is?" he asked.

There was some maturity in Kikuchi-san's voice. "I don't really know what goes on in your head, but…" After a pause, she said with some relief, "You're a really good person."

"Absolutely. Mizusawa is a nice guy." I felt that way pretty strongly, too, so I jumped in to agree.

I meant to have said that with sincerity and feeling, but for some reason, Mizusawa was scowling. "Hmm, as a ladies' man, being called a 'nice guy' or a 'good person' doesn't really have a positive meaning…"

"What's with that logic…?"

Then he said, "Well, I'm serious when it comes to Aoi, so I guess I'm good with that." Then he smiled like a young boy and tipped his glass back.

Well, isn't he playing it cool? It's always juice he's drinking, right?

"I told you, right? Every day is like a game for me, and I can manage without trying. I just kind of get what I want, and I've never been able to get serious."

These problems Mizusawa was dealing with—maybe, if I were to borrow Ashigaru-san's words, you would call that karma.

"…I think that helped some part of me have faith in myself." His expression seemed to conceal determination, with apparent confidence that ran deeper than his words. "But that didn't work on her. It was like she knocked me down a peg and rejected the way I'd always been. It was frustrating, but—I thought she was so interesting."

He'd finally found someone he couldn't reach.

"Well, of course, I'm still just in high school, so I might meet an even better woman in the future."

Ever since he'd told her his feelings at the camp during summer vacation—

Though he was more detached and cooler than anyone, the heat of his passion was directed toward just one person.

*　　*　　*

"But I can get serious right now. So I want to treasure that feeling."

Then Mizusawa bowed at me and Kikuchi-san. "So for once, I've got a request for you, Fumiya."

"...And what's that?"

It was really unusual for him to say something like this. I didn't even have to think back to know I was the one always asking him for things. That's not good. Thinking about it now, it meant I had a debt to him that couldn't be repaid so easily.

So I prepared myself to listen. But what popped out of Mizusawa's mouth was not quite what I had expected.

"Well, I have a sneaking suspicion that there's something that just you and maybe Kikuchi-san know about Aoi—something that I don't."

"!"

His gaze was fixed on me, with none of the teasing that had been there before.

"—Will you tell me what it is?"

With that, he struck right to the core of this discussion.

**　*　*　**

After a few minutes, I set down my now-empty glass.

When Mizusawa had asked me that, I'd taken a little time to think about what I should do. After all, this wasn't just my problem.

"...So hey," I just barely managed to say.

Mizusawa, however, was acting cool as usual, even though he'd just told us about his feelings. But I wondered if getting all that out had felt good, in a way.

"What's up, Fumiya?" he said.

"You're right that Hinami and I have a lot of secrets, or like…some things we're hiding."

"Ha-ha-ha. I bet." Mizusawa was back to his usual detached and easygoing manner, but there was still a serious light deep in his eyes. "But I don't know if it's something I can just tell you…you know?"

"Well, that's pretty fair."

Getting into someone's business, trying to change something there, came with a responsibility that couldn't be borne by an individual. And the responsibility was even greater when you didn't have that person's permission.

"True, I think you're right. This isn't something you can get permission for, and if you talked about it to someone who wasn't prepared, they'd just get burned. They wouldn't be able to deal with her feelings or what bad things might happen to her… But you know."

Then Mizusawa met my eyes with determination.

"Then she's going to remain alone forever, isn't she?"

The sincerity in his eyes made me feel something like horror.

I didn't get the sense that he had trouble taking on responsibility or feared knowing—all he had was consideration for Hinami. Or maybe the feeling he had now was a pure determination to push their relationship.

I think it was the resolution of a guy who knew what he wanted and was going after it.

Mizusawa had far fewer clues than me or Kikuchi-san—all he really had was his affection for her as he struggled to reach what lay deeper and continued to try to reach out.

But that hadn't been enough to get him there.

"Ahh…yeah."

While I felt Mizusawa's passion, I was thinking.

If an individual wanted to live alone, as an individual—then they didn't have to let anyone get too close to them. But that meant they couldn't overstep with anyone, either.

If you shouldered all responsibility yourself, then you could live freely. You wouldn't rely on anyone, but you wouldn't be bound by anyone, either.

"I think Hinami and I believe that the individual is the individual... We take responsibility for ourselves, but that means we don't want others overstepping our boundaries. I think that's been our approach to life."

Fundamentally, Hinami and I had both chosen that life of our own volition.

"That's... Yeah, I can get that," Mizusawa said.

"So...I don't have the right to talk about Hinami without her permission." That would be willfully broadening my interpretation of the rights I had.

"So I can take it you won't say?"

According to my logic, then yeah.

The individual was the individual. It would be unreasonable to disclose her secrets without her permission, to conspire with others to intrude more deeply into her heart. So I couldn't tell. That should have been my conclusion.

Should have been.

In Sewing Room #2, Kikuchi-san had thrown my heart into confusion. And when all those emotions had come bubbling up then, they had connected to the life goal etched into my heart:

To bring color to Aoi Hinami's life.

So then I...

"If I tell you everything now, that means I'm not playing as an individual anymore. I've always fought one-v-one."

"...Yeah, huh," Mizusawa said with resignation.

"...But..." If I did step down from that arena—if I did intrude on the rights of another.

I would have to put the transgression into more specific words.

That was what this unease I had was really about, more than whether I would say it or not.

So I drew in a breath, and as if making a declaration to the vague norms drifting around in the world—

"—I think of Hinami as someone special. That's why I'm going to tell you about her now, without her permission."

It was such a senseless, selfish declaration.

I also respected the individualism we shared, but I wanted to have more than that.

So I would infringe on her rights, precisely because she was someone I cared about.

Those were the incomprehensible feelings that I put into words.

"...Ha-ha-ha-ha!" Mizusawa laughed out loud. Kikuchi-san seemed a little sad, but she was smiling with kind understanding.

Mizusawa's laughter eventually settled. "God, you're weird."

"Well, I can agree with that." Feeling a weight off my shoulders, I laughed, too.

* * *

Less than an hour later.

"Well, that's about half what I expected, half worse than expected. RIP to me, I guess."

I'd told Mizusawa about what had happened.

"I didn't know normies said that, too...," I murmured.

My interest in irrelevant details aside, I'd just talked about meeting Hinami through *Atafami* and her teaching me how to play the game of life—including the part where all her effort had been to prove that she was right. Also, that Hinami had been trying to test her theory on me. Those three things.

"Oh well, that makes sense," Mizusawa said.

"It does?" I was surprised.

Sounding also sentimental, Mizusawa said, "Just thinking that I was drawn to her because she's an enigma." He was being very blunt as he gazed at the clear water in his glass. There was that single-minded heat I'd come to expect in the emotions he expressed.

"...Oh."

"Besides...if that's what it was, that explains how she doesn't show what she really feels to anyone, or the kind of scary level of effort she puts in, right?"

I nodded. Thinking of it now, when we'd met, I hadn't understood anything about her intentions or motivation. Once I'd started unraveling it, it was all connected by one thread.

But I still didn't know how she had gotten like that.

"So that means, like—won't *Atafami* be the key to the surprise?" Mizusawa said, bringing the discussion back around.

Before coming to know Hinami more deeply, our first priority was to show her a good time.

I wasn't sure whether we'd nailed down all the prerequisites, but since we'd shared the important points, we started to discuss the surprise again.

"Which means...an original video game...or something?" Kikuchi-san offered her ideas as well. She was amazing, really and truly.

Not because she was doing this in front of a guy who didn't know Hinami the way we did—she was making suggestions for a girl her boyfriend had just said was special. If Kikuchi-san was sitting here like, *The truth is, Tachibana-kun is special to me...*, then I'd lock myself in my bedroom for the next ten years.

"Well, sure, if you could make that happen, then it'd be great, but...,"

Mizusawa said like he didn't know what to do with that. He was probably avoiding disrespecting the idea, since it was Kikuchi-san's, but he was a realist at his core, so it was hard for him to agree to something with low chances of happening.

"Yeah...you probably can't make a video game so easily...," I said.

It wasn't like I knew a lot about how to make games, either, but having lived on the Internet for many years, I had a basic sense for things like that. Even if you used something like a crowdfunding service, it would be pretty difficult for us to complete one on our own.

"Hmm. If we at least had someone who knew a lot about the subject," Mizusawa said like he was talking to himself.

That gave me an idea. "...Maybe..."

My involvement with Kikuchi-san had helped give me the confidence to expand my world.

Maybe there was a relationship in that world that would be able to make that happen.

"You have an idea?" Mizusawa asked.

"Well, I don't know if that person could make it himself...but he might be able to introduce us to someone," I said.

That was when Kikuchi-san got it. "Oh...maybe he could have an acquaintance or something." She seemed honestly glad.

Well, his business was more *playing* games, so I didn't know if he would be able to help out directly. But I thought he might know some people who were involved in making them.

"Huh? What? Am I missing something?" Mizusawa said.

"Hmm, yeah, I wonder." This was fun, being one step ahead of him for once.

"Hey, Fumiya..."

"Actually, I know this guy, a pro gamer called Ashigaru-san—" And so I told him about what had happened at the offline meetups, and my relationships in that area.

Mizusawa nodded along. "Gotcha. A pro gamer would be a little closer to the business of video games and engineers and stuff… Well, it's got more possibilities than just us looking."

"Right?!"

And so once again, I was using what I'd gained over the past six months or so to move forward to my goal, bit by bit.

The time had flown by since beginning life-strategy meetings with Hinami. During that time, I'd seen her hidden side many times. And I'm sure that there, I'd gotten a glimpse of what she loved in the real sense, and not just "formalities."

So then I would use that not to try to expose her or pry into her business—I would use it to make her happy.

Heh, sorry, Izumi, but the one to make Hinami happiest will be me.

* * *

The discussion reached a lull.

"…Kikuchi-san is taking a while."

"Yeah."

Kikuchi-san had left the room to use the facilities, but it had been about ten minutes, and she hadn't come back.

"I'm gonna go check on her—"

Then the moment I stood up from the sofa—I heard voices from outside the room.

"Whaaat?! So Tomozaki-kun confessed to you?!"
"…s, …it was."

They were fragments of conversation. It was completely obvious that I was the subject of their gossip.

"Ah, I think…Gumi-chan got her."

"Ha-ha-ha. Don't worry about that, Fumiya," Mizusawa said with amusement. Glaring at him, I slumped back into the sofa.

From there, I noticed Mizusawa staring at me. "Which reminds me, Fumiya."

"Yeah?"

"Thanks."

"Huh? Where's this coming from?" I asked back.

The corners of Mizusawa's lips turned up a little, and his voice grew a little warm. "I mean, like. Well, I said I like Aoi, and you said she's special."

"Uh-huh."

"That's reason enough for me to try to know about her, and maybe that's reason enough for you to tell someone...but that's not a reason for you to tell me, is it?"

"...Ah." That was true—he was right.

I wouldn't tell the truth about Hinami so casually with just anyone who shared that determination to know her. I mean, I would be way out of bounds—I'd be giving someone else permission to get into Aoi Hinami's business.

"And that means, like—you trusted me," Mizusawa said with an irritating smirk. He was really striking at the core of the matter, which was what made it so irritating.

"Urk..."

"Wait—do you see me as your best friend?"

"Sh-shut up."

"Oh, what, are you shy now? Say it, c'mon, say it," he egged me on. He was loving this.

"I-I'm not gonna say it."

"Why not?" he asked with another smirk, and I looked inside myself for the words. He kinda had a point.

I mean, if he's asking if that's how I think of him..., I considered, and then I realized something. I didn't know where it came from, but I told the reasons I felt that way anyway. "A real best friend...won't have to say out loud that they're your best friend! Probably!"

Mizusawa stared at me for a moment. "…Hmm." Eventually, he smiled like a little kid, as if that convinced him. Then he clapped a hand on my shoulder. He sounded proud, but he was definitely trying to mess with me as he said:

"True enough. All right, then I'll be continuing to count on you—*Fumiya*."

3

Mastering Gadabout enables you to switch to a surprisingly strong job class

It was the Saturday a few days after that.

The members of Hinami's birthday planning committee had assembled again for a meeting, but...

"Mizusawa-senpai and Nanami-senpai—and now there's Nakamura-senpai and Yuzu-senpai, too?!" My little sister's eyes were sparkling as she stood at the entranceway of our house.

Apparently, my house was now the place to make plans. After getting together at Kitayono Station, the seven members of the planning committee came to gather at my house. *Wait, haven't I seen this before?*

My sister had come to greet us at the entrance, but her manners are so bad they're actually kinda cute. When she didn't know someone, she completely ignored them and didn't address them at all. Specifically, that was Tama-chan and Kikuchi-san. And there was also Takei, technically, but he's Takei. Ignoring him is good manners, IMO.

"Heya, Zakki! Thanks for having us over!" Izumi casually returned my sister's greeting—which reminded me. Didn't she say she had been in the badminton club with my sister?

"Yuzu-senpai! We've missed you!"

My sister was attached to Izumi. *This is the first time I've ever seen my sister actually being nice with someone.*

But getting a good look at them side by side, they had kind of similar hairstyles and stuff. Maybe my little sister was actually wanting to emulate

a fashionable senpai. If that's what it was, then it was cute. Even if plenty about her wasn't.

And so as I waited for everyone to come inside, I introduced my sister to those she didn't know. "Umm, next to Mimimi is Natsubayashi-san from the volleyball club, and the big guy is Takei…"

"Oh! Natsubayashi-senpai, I've seen you in the gym!"

"I've seen you, too. So you are Tomozaki's little sister?"

"I-I'm glad we could be introduced!"

"Me too!" Takei cut in to say hello.

I was getting nervous watching, because I would have to introduce someone else next.

"And this is—" I prompted Kikuchi-san to come forward.

"—my girlfriend, Kikuchi-san."

Time stopped for my sister as silence passed. It was as if time magic had been cast for those few seconds. Although, Kikuchi-san only casts white magic, so I probably have myself to blame for that one.

"…………What? You mean a girl who is your friend, right?"

"No, I don't mean it like that… I mean like we're dating."

"Uh, okay… A girlfriend who you're dating…"

Then my sister froze.

And then we waited for yet another powerful time spell to wear off, just over ten seconds.

"………Mooom! Bro just…!"

"Huh? …Fumiya has a girlfriend? Is there a snowstorm today? An earthquake? We have to prepare for some disaster!"

They were making such a big deal of it, and their jokes didn't even make sense. My face was starting to twitch. *What do I do? This is humiliating.*

But then—

"U-um!" Kikuchi-san called out, summoning her courage. "I-I'm Fuka Kikuchi! I'm dating Fumiya-kun!"

Once again, my sister froze like she was experiencing an overflow error.

"...Mooooom! A pretty girl is calling him Fumiya-kun!!"

"Ahh! Is it a meteorite?! I've got to give her a proper hello before it hits..."

"Never mind, okay?!" I yelped. "You don't have to come out here! G-guys, let's go to my room now."

Kikuchi-san's remark had thrown my household into further uproar, and I had the feeling that her saying anything more would just be more oil on the fire.

"I-I'm sorry, Fumiya-kun, it's my fault that..." It seemed Kikuchi-san felt responsibility about this that she really didn't need to feel.

"No...those two are just weird. Don't worry about it," I reassured her. With my mom and sister freaking out, I got everyone into the house. Then the eight of us went up the stairs to my room.

"Ah-ha-ha. Your family's always so funny, huh, Brain?"

"Yeah, I'm glad you're having such a good time..."

As Mimimi teased me, we started up the meeting in my room.

* * *

"'Kay, so then everyone's decided what they're doing for the surprise?" Mizusawa said.

Mimimi nodded. "You got it!" She must have grown since the last time, as she wasn't searching for any porn DVDs I might own. Just like me. I'd moved them from my math folder into the cloud.

Mimimi followed up with "Now to just actually do it!"

"We've decided what it is we're going to do, too," I replied.

"Hmm, we've decided on what we're doing, too, but we're struggling a little with the details...," Izumi said with a little groan. But she zipped right past that to move on with the meeting. "Well, more importantly, the main event for today! Let's decide where we're going for the trip!"

Yep—the main goal of the meeting that day was to decide on our destination. I joined Tama-chan in her hmming as I started racking my brain.

"I wonder where would be good? It's got to be someplace Aoi would like, huh...," said Tama-chan.

"Hmm. The first thing I can think of really is...cheese?" Izumi answered her.

You don't really see those two talking together, but I felt like they were meshing fairly naturally. Like the time with Kikuchi-san, Izumi is good at getting close to people.

"But even if we're starting there, where would we go? ...A farm?" Mimimi said. It sounded like that idea didn't really click with her.

"Yeah, that's iffy, huh," Izumi said with a frustrated noise as she tilted her head.

Well, if you're talking about what Hinami likes, then it's cheese. But that's better for a present or surprise—not actually going somewhere. We couldn't be going to a farm, or a cheese workshop, or a cheese museum for her birthday.

"What do we do...?" Izumi said like she was at a loss. But this was way too early for despair.

"...Yeah, huh." I was thinking about Hinami, but I was also thinking about myself. My hobbies were similar to hers, and so was the way I thought.

If you assumed that my own idea of fun was reliable, then I figured my feelings would be a good point of reference to think about her.

"Aoi seemed pretty tired, so how about a hot spring?" Tama-chan offered.

Mimimi tilted her head at that. "Come on, she's not an old man."

"Then why not go to Destiny Land? Cliché, but classic," Izumi said.

"Well, that would be the safe choice," said Mizusawa breezily. "But I figure Aoi's been a bunch of times before... What if she shows us around instead?"

"T-true…"

"But amusement parks are cool, right?!" Takei offered loudly. He's got a habit of reacting to things like amusement parks, video games, and shiny trading cards, so it really is easy to win him over… *Wait, hmm?*

"Amusement parks, video games…" Something about the list of Takei's habits that I'd made up stuck with me. The terms that had come to mind connected, and I felt like something was about to emerge there. The interesting place that I'd been wanting to go was—

"…Oh!"

Then I had a flash of inspiration. It was kinda like, *What a way to get that idea*, but I wasn't going to question it.

"Did you come up with an idea?" Kikuchi-san hadn't talked much before, but now she was looking to me to take the lead.

L-leave it to me! I'm feeling a little pressure from your expectations, but I really think this is a good idea.

"—Want to try going to Yontendo World?"

"Ohh…I see." Mizusawa reacted immediately to my suggestion, saying, "That might be a good idea." He seemed to get what I was trying to say. As expected of Mizusawa.

"Yontendo… Wait, Brain, isn't that the company of that *Atafami* game you like?" Mimimi said. Kikuchi-san understood what I was after as well, and her eyes widened.

"Umm…it'll take a bit to explain, but…" So I explained my intentions, careful not to touch on Hinami's secret. "You know Hinami likes video games, right? So that 'hexactly' she says a lot also comes from a game…"

"Ohh, really?" Mimimi said.

I nodded. "So I tried talking about it with her, and it seems like she actually likes *Atafami* quite a lot."

"Huh? Does she?" Nakamura tilted his head.

Ah, this is bad. It wouldn't be strange for Nakamura to have talked about *Atafami* around Hinami. If she had pretended not to know, then that might kind of be inconsistent with what I was saying. In fact, I think that right after I'd had that *Atafami* match with Nakamura, Hinami had still been maintaining the story that she didn't play it at all.

"Umm, well, maybe she started recently? But apparently, she's pretty into it."

"Ahh...well, I figure she'd talk about that sort of thing with you. Y'know, given your future pro gaming career." Mizusawa knew all about our secret, so he backed me up nicely there. It really is amazingly reassuring to have him on your side.

"Y-yeah, basically."

"And that's why the Yontendo World at Unlimited Space Japan, aka USJ... Look, here!" And then I went back through my search history—I'd been looking it up in the hopes of going sometime myself—and showed my phone screen to everyone.

"Ohhh...," said Nakamura.

It's like the world of a video game materialized in real life; anyone who loved video games would love to visit. You could actually meet the characters and experience attractions that get you into the games as well, like racing and a world tour and stuff.

At the very least, if you love Yontendo or *Atafami*, just seeing this image was enough to get you excited about the theme park—actually, I was already feeling it. That's Yontendo World.

"Ohhh! ...This is more amazing than I thought." Mimimi was in awe.

"This is that thing they made recently, right?" Izumi said in a bouncy tone.

"Oh yeah, I haven't gone to USJ since this was made. Looks fun." Nakamura agreed with the others. I felt like everyone's opinions were coming together. Like, Nakamura was kind of talking more than usual, and his eyes were sparkling as he looked at the screen. He really likes video games, too, huh.

"I—I think that's a good idea, too! It's like, um...I think Hinami-san might really enjoy herself there." Kikuchi-san seemed to understand things at a level deeper than the rest.

Takei, meanwhile, seemed to understand things three levels more shallowly than everyone else. "I'd love to go to USJ!" he cried.

Hmm, then this could work out.

"A-all right, are we good with this?" I asked.

"There's no point in us taking forever to pick where we're going, so sounds fine to me. Any objections?" Mizusawa asked.

"Nope!"

"No objections!"

"N-no objections!" said Kikuchi-san, who was new at this. With that, the location was settled.

"Aaaall right! So then for the Aoi birthday mission, our goal point is USJ in Osaka! Countin' on y'all for the Happy Hinami Arc in Yontendo World!" Mimimi used Mimimese to playfully get everyone excited. Cheers, applause, and whistling and stuff rose up around me, along with overexcited chattering and fooling around.

By the way, Nakamura was the one whistling with his fingers. Why is it that the most intimidating normies all whistle? Is it hereditary or something?

"Awww, this is so great! …But you really do know a lot about Aoi, huh, Brain!" Mimimi said.

Her remark startled me a little. "Y-yeah, I guess." I glanced meaningfully at Kikuchi-san and Mizusawa as the discussion moved along.

* * *

It was a little over an hour later.

"All right, folks, we've got a plan!" Mimimi jotted down notes in the notebook she was using to record proceedings—it was overflowing with doodles of some mystery mascot character—as she summarized what we'd talked about. "First, we meet up at Tokyo Station and take the Shinkansen to Osaka. We buy the tickets, of course, and then we go have fun at USJ!"

"Oh yeah, we haven't decided who'll buy Aoi's ticket," Mizusawa realized.

Tama-chan raised her hand. "Oh, I'll buy it!"

"Okay, thanks for covering that."

And so we decided roles, and Mimimi reviewed all the notes she'd put together. "So we stay over at a hotel close to USJ, have a surprise party there, and Aoi cries!"

"That's not much of a plan…"

"Don't sweat the details, Brain!"

Then Izumi raised her hand. "Oh, one question!"

"Yes, cutie Yuzu-chan!"

"What sort of dinner are we having that night? Since we have the opportunity, I think it would be nice to get something Aoi likes!"

Then Mimimi suddenly got evasive. "Ahh, umm…" She started glancing over at Tama-chan like she was trying to communicate silently. "Sorry! Well, uh, you know…just leave that stuff to us!"

"Huh? …Oh! R-roger!" Izumi said like she had figured it out, and her questioning ended without pinning down more details. Well, it's not good to pry too much, but Mimimi's reaction just now—if she wanted to leave the dinner to them, that meant Mimimi's team's surprise for Hinami would be something related to dinner.

Huh, I see.

That meant probably—almost definitely—that the surprise Mimimi's team was organizing was related to cheese. Hinami totally did love cheese, so I'd leave it to them to handle that.

It was evening.

"Thanks for having us over!"

We had dropped the discussion around the latter half, mainly playing video games, cards, and board games and stuff to end the meeting that day. Now I was with my mother and sister at the front door sending everyone off.

"Come by again sometime!!" my sister said.

"Mm-hmm. We'll come again, Zakki!" Izumi replied.

"Okay!" Getting a response from someone she admired seemed to brighten my sister's mood.

My mother leaned over and started whispering with my sister, and then something in her eyes changed. They nodded at each other. *What are they talking about, I wonder?*

Everyone made their farewells, then went out from the entranceway, leaving me, my sister, and my mother behind. By the way, I was facing the door right then, but I felt eyes burning into me.

"So, Bro…"

"Fumiya…"

"Y-yes…?" I replied with trepidation and turned around to find two insatiably curious creatures.

"When did you get a girlfriend?!"

"Why didn't you say anything, Fumiya?! And she's so cute!"

"Yeah! How can you get such a cute girlfriend, Bro?!"

"You can talk to me if you're doing something bad! If you turn yourself in, Fumiya, then I'll go with you!"

All I could do was stand there as they rambled at me.

* * *

That evening, I was looking up things about USJ and Yontendo World on my phone when I got a reply on LINE from Ashigaru-san. "…Oh."

I tapped the notification and checked what it said.

[*I see, I get your situation.*

I know a video game programmer—do you want to try talking to him? I could introduce you someplace on Sunday afternoon.]

"That would help so much…"

He moved the discussion so smoothly—I should've expected that from a famous pro gamer. Maybe part of the reason he was making the time for me was because I was nanashi, but I was still really grateful to him.

I swiftly sent the message to the LINE group for our surprise organization team. By the way, Mizusawa had been the one to suggest and make the group chat for efficiency's sake. Just what I'd expect from Mizusawa. He plays the game of life so well.

Then before long, I got back messages from the other two.

[If it's a Sunday, then I'm free tomorrow or the week after next] came from Mizusawa.

Kikuchi-san's message read, *[I can go any time!]*

"Hmm."

So if we were going to make everyone's schedules match, that would make it either the next day or the Sunday two weeks later.

Well, we did have a month until Hinami's birthday, but—if we were going to be talking about making a game, the week after next wouldn't leave enough time for production.

After I checked the date with Kikuchi-san and Mizusawa, I replied to Ashigaru-san so that we could make plans as early as possible.

A reply came less than twenty seconds later.

[So then how about tomorrow at three, at Itabashi Station?]

"*All right. Then please arrange that for us*...and send."

The quick response was just what you'd expect from a competent working adult. He was so cool. After I sent my reply and closed my phone, I connected my charger and leaned back in the chair I was sitting on.

Right now, I was being rejected by Hinami.

But even so—I was using my time to make her happy.

I still didn't really understand myself why that was.

*　　*　　*

I thought back on how Hinami had been in Sewing Room #2 and everyone else's image of who she was.

With our class, she had always operated the character Aoi Hinami as the player Aoi Hinami. But just with me, she would take off her mask and descend from her position as player into the world of characters to talk with me—or so I had thought.

But maybe the truth was that wasn't what had been happening.

What if, even in our place—even in Sewing Room #2—what if she'd just been sticking the controller into the character called NO NAME from her dimension as the player Aoi Hinami?

Where were her real feelings, with no "formalities" involved?

Where was the Aoi Hinami who was neither a perfect heroine nor NO NAME?

＊ ＊ ＊

It was the next day, Sunday.

I'd taken Kikuchi-san and Mizusawa to Itabashi.

Itabashi was the station where I'd come with Hinami before—this was where Ashigaru-san lived.

"Umm, oh, it's over there." I found the café that Ashigaru-san had indicated and led the other two there.

"Ashigaru-san? That's what he's called, right?" said Mizusawa. "He's a pro gamer, right? He makes a living with video games."

"Yeah."

"...Huh. That's an unusual way to make a living."

"Well...maybe it is off the beaten path. Although, I've decided to aim for the same thing."

"Ha-ha-ha, oh yeah."

It was unusual for Mizusawa to be interested in someone he hadn't met yet, I mused as I took the crosswalk to the entrance. I went in to find Ashigaru-san wasn't there yet, so I decided to just get a seat and—

"Hey, nanashi-kun," a voice called out from behind, making me leap aside.

"Whoa?!"

I turned around to see Ashigaru-san. He must have arrived at the café at just about the same time as us.

"H-hey, if you're there, then say something, please."

"Uh, I did just say something, though?"

"...True."

Seeing me get argued down in less than a second, Mizusawa and Kikuchi-san giggled.

Mizusawa quickly grasped the situation, though, and he faced Ashigaru-san with his usual smile. He almost seemed used to this. "Nice to meet you. I'm Fumiya's friend, Takahiro Mizusawa."

"Fumiya? Oh, you mean nanashi-kun. I'm... It's a little embarrassing to introduce myself like this to someone who isn't a gamer, but I use the name Ashigaru. Nice to meet you."

"Yeah. Of course, we came to talk to you about the surprise today, but I'd like to ask you about a lot of other things as well, if I can. I'm glad to meet you, too."

"Mm...yeah, sure."

Mizusawa was chatting away in a fluid stream just like he always did, even with Ashigaru-san—he was even kind of guiding the conversation. Where did he learn those communication skills? Are the rumors that he works a sketchy nighttime job true?

"Umm, and who's the girl with you?" Ashigaru-san looked over at Kikuchi-san, apparently attempting to divert the discussion from Mizusawa.

Kikuchi-san glanced at me hesitantly. *Umm, well, right now, she's probably thinking about that sort of thing. Yeah, I know that she's like that sometimes.*

And so I indicated Kikuchi-san with the palm of my hand. "Umm, basically, this is Kikuchi-san...my girlfriend."

"Huh?!" Ashigaru-san yelped, unusually for him.

Kikuchi-san's face went red—or that's what I expected anyway. But for some reason, she was nodding like she was kind of satisfied. *Uh-oh, Kikuchi-san is starting to get used to these situations. But I want her to stay shy forever.*

"So you're nanashi-kun's... I see. Nice to meet you," said Ashigaru-san.

"I-I'm Kikuchi! Umm, ah...i-it's good to meet you." Kikuchi-san tensed up again as she greeted him with a bow.

Ashigaru-san gave a mature smile. "Then for now, how about we sit over there?"

"R-right!"

As I followed Ashigaru-san, I tried asking the question that had been on my mind. "Umm...so what about that programmer?"

Since we were here to talk about an original game, we were going to be meeting a game programmer who was an acquaintance of Ashigaru-san's. But right now, he was nowhere to be seen.

"Actually, I told him we're meeting in half an hour. I know nothing about this, so I thought it might be best to get the rundown from you first."

"Oh...I see."

That was a very grown-up response. I could see he was an adult juggling multiple responsibilities. Being a pro gamer doesn't mean anything goes as long as you're good at games—he had to have skills in that area as well.

A few minutes after taking our seats, we all ordered drinks, and we started off with just chatting.

"Anyway, this is surprising," Ashigaru-san said.

"Huh? What is?" I asked.

He looked at Mizusawa and Kikuchi-san. "I was thinking, *Oh, so this is what nanashi-kun's friend and girlfriend are like,*" he said in an easygoing manner.

"Ha-ha-ha, so what are we like?" Mizusawa responded, just as easygoing. A battle of the easygoing had begun.

"Well, um, you're not exactly gamer types."

"Ahh, maybe that's true. Actually, though..." Sounding a little more performative than usual, Mizusawa said, "I'm the type to see life as a game, so."

Ashigaru-san fell into thought. "Hmm, I see. That's interesting. From that perspective, you could say everyone's a gamer. I mean, there's actual gamers, and then everyone else is grappling with other things, too."

"Huh? Oh...yeah, maybe."

"Or maybe like," I added, "you could say that everything is a game, so long as it has some form of rules and results."

"Whoa, you too, Fumiya?" Mizusawa seemed taken aback by Ashigaru-san and me suddenly jumping into this logic, but I guess it's the nature of a gamer to consider this stuff to a tiresome degree. By the way, Kikuchi-san was watching us with a smile. She's very accepting.

"Thank you for waiting!"

And then the drinks we'd ordered arrived.

"Sorry, sorry, that discussion went off in a weird direction... So you want to make a video game, right?"

And so we shifted to the main subject at hand.

* * *

"Okay, so this is supposed to be a present...," Ashigaru-san muttered as he put his lips on the cup in front of him. I'd just basically explained how things had gone. By the way, Ashigaru-san was drinking hot chocolate. Not what I would have guessed.

"Yes. We were talking about how that was the best idea," I said.

"Mm-hmm. Well, yeah, from what you've told me, I do think she'd like it if you pulled it off..."

"Yeah." I showed I was listening.

Ashigaru-san's voice was always so clear, even though he often sounded like he was talking to himself. "Would you normally go that far?" he asked.

His fireball made Mizusawa burst into laughter. "Ha-ha-ha! He's got us there!"

"Um, well, I guess you have a point..." A little late, I nodded, too.

Now that he mentioned it, that was entirely true—you normally wouldn't go to the trouble to request a pro to make an original video game just for your classmate's birthday. Even with a girlfriend or boyfriend, you might start worrying it would freak them out. I still haven't celebrated Kikuchi-san's birthday yet, so I can't say, though.

"So then I guess this person is just that special? Or do popular kids at school like Mizusawa normally do stuff like that?"

"Ha-ha-ha! What's that supposed to mean?"

"Well, you're the type of guy I probably wouldn't have been friends with if I were in the same class as you, back in high school...," Ashigaru-san said, somewhere between joking and sincere.

A pleasant smile crossed Mizusawa's face. "You're honest, Ashigaru-san."

"Well, I am older. Plus, if I was all careful and polite, I'd be hard to talk to, right?"

"Yeah, this does make it easier." It seemed like Mizusawa was enjoying and amused by Ashigaru-san's frankness. Well, Mizusawa had been interested in him before they met. Does he like people who are a little different? Now that I think of it, he'd suddenly come up to me before and said stuff like *"You're a weird guy"* and *"I'm on your side."*

"Well, even with my friend group, you normally wouldn't go this far," Mizusawa said.

"Oh, really? Then why with this?"

"Hmm. Ashigaru-san, you asked if this person is special, right?"

"I did."

Stirring the iced coffee he'd ordered, Mizusawa said, "The one we're throwing a party for is a girl I like."

Again, he said it so easily.

Despite having already heard that just recently, Kikuchi-san's and my shoulders twitched. I mean, you won't get used to that sort of thing no matter how many times you hear it, right?

But Ashigaru-san maintained a more level tone than expected. "Huh. Is that right?"

Mizusawa looked kinda disappointed.

Hey, so is he trying to get a rise out of people, after all? Don't use those methods to try to surprise an adult you've only just met. "Mizusawa, you don't have to tell him that part," I said.

"And I don't have to keep it secret, right?"

"Well, that is true..." But I still didn't get why he would say it. Anyway, I was impressed he could say that over and over like there was nothing to it. For me, that would be an ultimate spell like Magic Burst that would consume all my MP to cast, but he was firing it off like a regular attack.

"So then...what about you two? Are you invested in Mizusawa-kun's love life?"

"Ahh, no, that's not why..." I shook my head.

Well, of course you would think that. I mean, since I was dating Kikuchi-san, and we were throwing this celebration for a girl—this certainly would look like a couple who was supporting Mizusawa's crush.

"Well...it's more that I really owe her a lot—she's given me things that I wouldn't be able to repay..."

"Hmm..."

"Umm, and you, Kikuchi-san?" I turned the discussion to Kikuchi-san, who hadn't really been talking much.

A little flustered, she said, "Y-yes! Umm, I...did something to her I shouldn't have... This isn't to atone, but, um, I want to make her happy."

"...I see." Having heard more or less everything from us, Ashigaru-san's expression finally turned serious. "So basically, this girl...is burdened with a lot of things, isn't she...?"

It was just a coincidence, but his words cut incredibly close to the core of the matter.

* * *

Then about half an hour later—

"Ohh, here he is. Hey, hey, thanks for today."

"Yeah, thanks, Ashigaru-san."

When the programmer arrived, Ashigaru-san stood from his chair to greet him, so we emulated him and stood as well.

"This is Endo-kun. He works at a game-production company... What they do is like subcontracting for some of Yontendo's software."

"Ahh, hi, nice to meet you."

Endo-san was probably in his midtwenties and dressed casually in what they call "creative's attire": a short black beard, glasses, and a white shirt and jeans. His short hair and clothes were sharp and neat, with an incredible aura of cleanliness. My first impression was that he seemed like a reliable working man.

His expression was always soft, and the little smile on his lips was rather distinctive.

"Umm, so for starters—this is the guy everyone's talking about: nanashi-kun." Ashigaru-san introduced me in a meaningful-sounding way.

I bobbed my head in a bow. "Nice to meet you. Umm, I'm nanashi, or Fumiya Tomozaki." I wasn't sure if maybe I should do what Ashigaru-san had done and just say my nickname, but well, since this was a request as Hinami's classmate Tomozaki, I decided to just introduce myself with my real name.

"Ohh, so you're nanashi-kun. I've heard about you. I'm Endo. I generally work as a programmer, and I develop some game apps and stuff on my own, too."

He's heard about me? What exactly has he heard...? Well, this was Ashigaru-san, so it couldn't have been anything bad. I told myself not to worry about it as I returned a bow.

"I'm nanashi-slash-Fumiya's friend, Takahiro Mizusawa." Casually absorbing the word *nanashi*, which he'd probably only just heard that day, Mizusawa greeted him politely. Mizusawa really does have the skills of a working adult. Is he really a high schooler?

"U-umm! I'm Fumiya-kun's... Um! Wait, I mean...I'm Fuka Kikuchi." Kikuchi-san started copying Mizusawa's introduction template and was about to say what our relationship was, but she managed to avoid the unnecessary announcement in the nick of time. Even if she was getting used to being introduced as my girlfriend, she apparently didn't have the courage to declare it to someone she'd just met.

Endo-san looked over the three of us and smiled. "We've got a nice crowd lined up here...but can I take it today, you're here to talk about work?"

"Y-yes! Actually..." And so I started off by giving him an outline of the occasion. "A friend of ours has a birthday party coming up..."

I explained that she liked games, especially *Atafami*, that we wanted to make a similar original game, and that we wanted to something high-quality enough to make her happy. So basically, our ideal scenario was to make a game that was like *Atafami* that she could actually enjoy. I was not mentioning for now that said girl was my gamer friend Aoi, since that would make things complicated.

Endo-san jotted down notes in a black, leather-bound notebook, then capped his fountain pen and tap-tapped it on the blank space. "That's a pretty difficult request."

"O-oh yeah?"

"By the way, when was the deadline...er, the girl's party again?"

"Umm..."

"It's March nineteenth," Mizusawa answered. As expected of the guy with a crush on Hinami—he had the fastest finger on that question.

"Hmm, about your conditions... First, fighting games are really hard to make."

"Oh...they are, huh." I'd just been wondering that myself.

"Yeah. It takes a lot of man-hours to make one, from the design, character motion, and sound effects to game balance, so it's pretty hard to make one solo...and absolutely impossible in one month."

"Oh..."

All our faces fell.

"Yeah, no surprise there. But I think you can figure something out with your ideas," Ashigaru-san pressed.

"Hey...don't put me on the spot here," said Endo-san, and he fell into thought with a "hmm."

"S-sorry for asking for something so unreasonable...," I said.

"No, no, Ashigaru-san is always like this," Endo answered like he was used to it. "All right...then how about something like this, for example?" He was acting like he'd hit on something, making me instinctively lean forward in enthusiasm.

"You put in stages and characters like from *Atafami*, so you still have two players control characters to battle. You put hitboxes on the characters, but the moment you hit the other character...you get menu options instead of an action-based fight," Endo-san muttered as if he was organizing it in his head as he spoke.

While digesting what he said, I envisioned his idea. "Oh...I get it." I had the feeling I'd seen a system kind of like that before, like in an RPG or as a minigame in a party game.

"Then maybe it's like rock-paper-scissors. The winner is decided based on the option picked, and you damage the opponent. Rinse and repeat till someone wins. I think if you want an '*Atafami*-style' competitive game with a simple system like that, it's not impossible to make."

"Yeah...I kind of get it."

"I see. It's true that if you make it like that, then you don't need the motion of a fighting game. All you need are the basic parts of a video game—moving the character and the hitbox—right?" Ashigaru-san confirmed with Endo-san.

"That's right." Endo-san nodded. "And if it's just a thing for your friends, then you're fine to borrow the actual graphics from *Atafami*, too..."

His bold proposal seemed to amuse Mizusawa. "Ha-ha-ha! You're okay with the gray zone, huh!"

"If it's something like that, I think I could manage it in one month."

Kikuchi-san beamed brightly. "O-oh, really?! That's great!"

It seemed like we were all in agreement and everything was resolved now, but something inside me still felt off.

"Umm...yeah, that is great, but..."

Noticing my lack of enthusiasm, Mizusawa asked me, "Something's not quite right to you?"

I got the vague sense that something was off; searching for the words, I said, "Umm...I think that games can be broadly divided into two elements."

"Oh, are we about to hear nanashi-kun's theory on games? Sounds interesting." Ashigaru-san watched me closely.

"Ahh, no, no, please don't get your hopes too high..."

"Nah, we're expecting great things from you, Fumiya."

"Hey..."

Though I didn't like the way they were looking at me, I explored my thoughts as I spoke. "In a video game, there's the core content—like the system or rules—and then the exterior, like the characters and UI, right?"

"True."

"I see. Yeah, that's right."

"I guess...?"

"Umm, what do you mean...?"

There was Endo-san, Ashigaru-san, Mizusawa, and Kikuchi-san. Judging from their reactions, they'd responded in order of their depth of knowledge about video games, and their levels of understanding were all completely different. *Hmm, then I've got to explain for Kikuchi-san.*

"Look, take *Atafami* for example. The system and rules are that you can do moves in different directions, like ground or air, and when you damage to the opponent, it knocks them way back. If you knock them all the way off-screen, you get closer to winning."

"Y-yes." Kikuchi-san was doing her best to keep her eyes up as she listened to me. She was probably thinking back on playing *Atafami* at my place.

"You also have characters that all look wildly different. You've got the ninja Found, you've got Foxy, you've got Lizard. But that has nothing to do with the system or rules, right?"

"Um…really?"

I see, so this wasn't making sense to her. So then how to explain?

As I was thinking about it, Ashigaru-san jumped in to lend me a hand.

"For example, what if Found became a blue stick person, Foxy was a red stick person, and Lizard was a green stick person? That wouldn't change the system and rules of the game at all, right?"

That metaphor helped Kikuchi-san understand. "Oh, I see! The game would still be about doing damage to win, huh!"

"But what about that?" Mizusawa was tilting his head.

"Umm, so like. As far as I know…" I thought back on what Hinami had said just after we'd met.

"…Hinami's the type to care more about rules and systems than the exterior of a game."

Mizusawa blinked in surprise.

This was the way NO NAME had thought ever since we first met.

A game with rules that are simple but deep is the best kind. That's why she thought the game of life was god-tier, why she could see what made an apparently kiddie game like *Oinko* interesting. It was also why she'd noticed the depth of a certain party game called *Atafami*.

"So…even if you make just the exterior like *Atafami*, if the gameplay is completely different, Hinami will probably be looking at the rules."

Then I realized that *"Hinami"* had popped out of my mouth multiple times, so I quickly explained for Ashigaru-san. "Oh, 'Hinami' is the name of the girl whose birthday it is." I'd kinda gotten worked up there.

Ashigaru-san nodded slowly few times and opened his mouth. It looked like Endo-san was watching to see what he would say. "I see... That makes things difficult."

"...Yes, that's true."

Yeah—if she was the type to value the rules of a game...

If we couldn't use the exterior to gloss over what was underneath, then we'd have to create something with high-quality gameplay in less than a month—a game with "rules that were simple but deep."

"There are tricks of the trade that can help you cheat on the graphics, but it's hard to do that for the gameplay. With fighting games especially," said Endo-san.

"Yeah." Ashigaru-san nodded.

"But, Fumiya, if we're making a game, then won't we be forced to compromise on that somewhat? Actually, based on my experience, just coming up with such an involved surprise is already good enough to let her know how you feel," Mizusawa chided me. He was looking at reality with a cool head.

He was right—maybe what Hinami cared about was the system and rules, but she already liked *Atafami*. And if you like a game, playing it will get you attached to the characters, too.

In that sense, the alternative idea—borrowing just the characters and making the gameplay more realistic—wasn't a bad one.

"There is less than a month, after all..." Kikuchi-san agreed with Mizusawa. Most likely, if you hadn't seen Hinami talking about games or rules, then you wouldn't really get it.

You wouldn't get just how fixated she was on rules and structure.

There was no way for them to understand that the rules were more important than anything to her.

"Yeah…" That was why I was thinking about this.

I wasn't just going to frantically insist that I knew this. If I wanted them to accept my suggestion, I had to get them to appreciate what was needed. In other words, I would use Aoi Hinami's methods to make something Aoi Hinami would enjoy.

There was the essence of a game, and then the exterior.

To be specific, this meant the rules and the graphics.

If I was going to help Hinami have the best birthday ever—if I was going to do what I wanted to do—I had to select the most realistic, the most effective ideas from the clues at hand right now.

If I was to do it my way and change the original conditions—

"…Oh." The light bulb was on.

"Do you have an idea, nanashi-kun?" Ashigaru-san asked.

I breathed in and out. "I'm sorry, this will mean wasting everything we've talked about until this point, but…"

While thinking about another game Hinami liked, I said:

"—What if it was a shooter?"

Endo-san and Ashigaru-san stared at me.

"Well, yes…if it was a simple 2D shooter, I do think that would be quite a bit less work, but…," Endo-san said, carefully choosing his words.

"Really?!"

"Why a shooter?" Ashigaru-san probed.

I was unsure of where to start, but I said, "Um, the truth is…there's a game she's almost as attached to as *Atafami*."

Mizusawa and Kikuchi-san looked surprised to hear that—of course, they were. I hadn't brought up those details when talking about Hinami with the two of them.

"She's attached to a shooter?"

I nodded.

"It's called *Go Go Oinko*."

Mizusawa and Kikuchi-san were still blank. But Ashigaru-san's eyes started sparkling brightly. "Ohh! *Oinko*! That's a girl with taste!"

As expected of a pro, he knew about *Oinko*. His gaze rose to the ceiling with nostalgia as he continued fondly, "The gameplay and story were both good... I think I remember... What was it again, that catchphrase of Oinko's? 'That's so correct, I think I've been hexed! Hexactly!' It was so cute."

" "Hexactly?!" "

Mizusawa and Kikuchi-san cried out in surprise at exactly the same time—I'd never seen them do that before.

"Huh, what...? What is it?" Ashigaru-san was surprised in turn.

Well, if you didn't know how Hinami was at school, it would be hard to guess why they were repeating a catchphrase in stereo. It was a real weird moment.

Mizusawa leaned out toward me. "So the game 'hexactly' comes from is a shooter?"

"Yep. Hexactly." I stuck out my finger at him, which Mizusawa smacked aside. Rude.

"Fumiya, don't be obnoxious."

"I think that would work!" Kikuchi-san was also super excited. I wasn't expecting that. *So she also associates 'hexactly' with Hinami, even though they haven't spoken that much.* Now that I was thinking about it, though, Hinami had casually declared it during her election speech, too. No matter how you think about it, that's going too far.

"There's possibilities, right?" I said, and the two of them nodded at each other. I think we all had a good feeling about this.

Ashigaru-san looked at the three of us with utter skepticism. "So this girl has really made *hexactly* her brand...," he said with a wry smile. With confidence, we answered, """Yes!"""

* * *

After that, we discussed where to take the game, and after sharing each of our views, our negotiation reached a head—or really, our negotiation finally got started for real.

"So...that's what it comes down to, after all," I said.

"Yes, indeed." Endo-san's smile was warm, but he nodded with an unwavering gaze. "We do this professionally—we have to get paid. It will be taking my time, after all."

Yes. It was the issue of money.

Even if he was the friend of a friend, this was his living. While he was managing our request, he wouldn't be able to do other work. So then the obvious way to take responsibility for that was to pay out enough to compensate. Of course, we'd talked about that beforehand as well, and we were prepared.

"But since you're a friend of Ashigaru-san's, and this doesn't need to be a commercial product, I can make it lower than usual."

"R-really?"

"Yes. Plus, you guys are high school kids. Depends on what your budget is, though..."

"Y-yes, of course." I wasn't used to conversations like this, and I was struggling. It was completely different from the typical way I'd communicate with classmates—I mean, this was a conversation involving profit and loss calculations and relating to money and time; I had no idea what I should say or how I should say it. The rules for this were just too different.

"Okay, so how do we want to do this?" Endo-san started off, throwing that question at me like a jab. Well, I had been talking like I was the coordinator here.

"Umm, s-so yeah…" I wasn't sure how to reply, but since I couldn't say nothing, I made a small remark to buy some time. But that would only give me a few seconds, and then I'd have to come up with some kind of response. *Ngh, what do I do?*

If I'm going to make a decision, then I should start by referencing what I get for my allowance. Probably not the best idea, but then—

"—Given the work and time required, just how much is typical for a request like this?"

Now *that* was someone who knew how to negotiate.

"Being that we're taking up your valuable time for work, we'd like to offer the maximum compensation, but of course, this is the first time we've tried something like this, so we don't even know where to start, really…" Mizusawa was saying all the right things eloquently one after another as if he'd thought it up beforehand.

Endo-san looked like Mizusawa's move surprised him, but then he put a hand on his chin and started to think. "Umm, what's typical? Um, let me see…"

Beside him, Ashigaru-san's eyes were also wide. It was as if that moment had changed the air around us.

How would I put it—Mizusawa was acting like that time when he'd been campaigning for the election at the school gates or making his candidate support speech at the gym. In formality-heavy conversations like this, he unfortunately might even be on par with Hinami.

"About…" Endo-san hesitated to say it directly; he scrawled the amount on a café napkin with his fountain pen instead. He presented it to me by handing it to me with a smile.

"…I see."

Well, roughly speaking, the sum would suck up about half a year's worth of the income from both my and Mizusawa's part-time jobs put together. Frankly speaking, it wasn't realistic. I passed it on to Mizusawa and Kikuchi-san. Seeing the number, Kikuchi-san's eyes went as round as if the number were in some foreign currency. Well, there is a possibility that Kikuchi-san typically uses white wings as her currency.

"Ah…" The negativity was apparent in Mizusawa's voice.

"Well"—Endo-san nodded—"that's rather tough for teenagers, huh. So if we decrease the quality a little and call the rest an Ashigaru-san discount, I could take it down to half this…but even that is expensive, huh?"

"…Yeah, that'll be tough." Mizusawa paused, but his response expressed a clear intention.

"I'm sorry, any less than that and I have to start worrying about food and rent, so I wouldn't be able to take the time… But a really basic free game isn't quite what you're imagining, is it?"

Mizusawa nodded. "Yes. So I would hope we could find a good compromise, but—" Expression serious, he began to waver. His long, thin fingers tapped slightly on the table, his lowered gaze scrutinizing the table and the contents of his own mind.

"…" Unbothered by the silence created by his pause, Mizusawa eventually focused his attention back and forth between Kikuchi-san and me. It didn't seem as if he was seeking help—in fact, it was as if he was searching for a clue.

After a while, his gaze stopped on me, and his lips curled in a smile.

"…Hmm?" I had a really bad feeling about this.

I was right about to ask the reason for that when Mizusawa started scheming. "Fumiya, this will mean you're gonna have to do just a liiittle bit of work for us, but that's okay, right?" He was acting like he was just checking.

"Huh?"

But he didn't wait to hear my reply; instead, he called both their names.

"—Well then, Endo-san, Ashigaru-san." Expressly using their names again was a pretty strong card to play in a conversation, and both of them seemed overwhelmed by it as they waited for Mizusawa to continue.

"We have a proposal for you." Mizusawa stuck up a finger and put on an expression of confidence. This was not how a high school kid acted in front of two adults. Ashigaru-san and Endo-san's eyes were wide and captured by Mizusawa's performance.

"Of course, this should be obvious by this point, but we're high school students, and frankly, we don't really have much money," Mizusawa said with levity and a slightly exaggerated sense of patheticness.

"Ah-ha-ha. For sure." Endo-san laughed. The vibe was comical and cute, softening the seriousness of what was being discussed.

And then it hit me.

What had just begun was a real negotiation.

"Yes, we have part-time jobs, but we're probably real poor compared to adults..."

"Ha-ha! I'm sure that's true."

Mizusawa was going through all the formalities while hiding his true intentions. This was probably a modestly high-level technique, gently sharing the core issues relating to both parties' interests, whether that was with regards to conditions or money. It was probably a vital skill in negotiation. Since he was the one going into that territory, he'd even gained the initiative.

But I would never have imagined where this speech from Mizusawa would suddenly start going.

"So...there is more or less a reason that we have no money."

"There is?"

"Yes." Mizusawa looked at me. "Nanashi-kun here has had a lot of things to buy lately. Do you know what they might be?"

"...No." Endo-san tilted his head at the sudden question. Was the pop-quiz format another one of Mizusawa's techniques? That reminded me, back during the election when he'd made a speech the school gates, he'd said something like *"And you there, in the glasses!"*

While making eye contact with me, Mizusawa grinned and said, "— It's streaming equipment."

Ashigaru-san and Endo-san nodded as if that made sense to them. I was just surprised.

It's true that I'd decided I would pursue a pro gaming career, and to that end, I'd made a Twitter account and decided that I would show up regularly at offline meetups. And I'd also considered posting videos myself or streaming live.

But I hadn't told that to Mizusawa.

Meaning Mizusawa was just guessing about all this—essentially, it was a bluff.

"He's still starting out right now—he's serious about becoming a pro gamer, but not familiar with it yet. He's only just getting all the equipment, getting started generating content on a consistent schedule, and gaining influence. He's right at the stage where he's about to go professional."

"Yeah. He's basically told me about that already." Ashigaru-san nodded.

Once he had confirmation, Mizusawa said, "So here we get to the subject at hand—" He clapped a confident hand on my shoulder.

"Endo-san, why not buy nanashi's future influence?"

That was when I understood what Mizusawa was trying to do.

"First of all, there's the game he plays, *Attack Families*. It's incredibly popular; it's got the largest number of players in Japan. And this guy has the number one online winrate in the country—a position he's defended for a while now. It's no overstatement, in a sense, to say he's the number one gamer in Japan." Mizusawa built up his logic, mixing a bluff with facts.

"I have heard about him…but hearing you put it that way, maybe he's a bigger deal than I thought." Maybe Endo-san sensed that this wasn't just some high schooler's idea of a joke. His expression turned serious, waiting for what Mizusawa said next.

"But the game of life isn't that easy." Mizusawa shrugged, brow furrowing. "Being a pro gamer means being in the business of popularity. Just being good at the game isn't enough. You have to have a little extra something."

"That's exactly right." Ashigaru-san nodded.

"It can be your appearance, your career history, or your age. All these things are judged as a whole, and that's what gets you popularity."

"Yeah. I agree with that." Endo-san nodded as well.

"Even people who are good at gaming—if they don't know how to talk to people, or they don't dress well, or they're just kinda boring, they often can't get popular from their skills alone." Then Mizusawa swept his gaze over at me and said, "But with nanashi—he seems like he'll be all right, don't you think?" He tossed the question to Endo-san, who nodded again.

Ashigaru-san seemed impressed.

"I see...," said Endo-san. "True, he does have the character, doesn't he?"

Mizusawa jabbed a finger at him. "Yes. Hexactly!"

"Ha! *Oinko*, huh," Ashigaru-san said, sounding pleased.

What the heck? This is the first time I've seen someone other than me or Hinami use "hexactly," and the first time I've seen anyone get it immediately. What a high-context moment.

Then Mizusawa gestured at me, as if I was a product he was proud to present. "He's the number one *Atafami* player in Japan, decently good at talking, he's got the looks—and most of all, he's still in high school. You can call him *the handsome high schooler and top* Atafami *player. He can chat, too!* Really, that's perfect as a slogan!"

"Ha-ha-ha! True." Ashigaru-san laughed out loud.

Please don't assign me a slogan without asking.

But when that topic had come up at the offline meetup, that thought *had* crossed my mind.

Put together the gaming skills I had and the abilities I'd gotten from Hinami, and I had several elements going for me.

"So you understand what I'm driving at, don't you?" Mizusawa had gotten warmed up, and there was a tempo to his speech now.

You could sense zeal and confidence in his expression, and it was changing the air at the table.

*　　*　　*

"If we take nanashi's social media and use it to advertise the game app you make, Endo-san, the effect will be substantial."

"...I see."

This had already gone beyond a discussion about a high school kid's birthday party—now it was like a business talk or a battle of words.

Endo-san nodded several times. So he wasn't *not* on board with this. But we were still lacking a deciding factor or something like that.

"Fumiya, you have nanashi's account, right? Can you open it now?"

"Huh? O-okay." I opened up my phone app, swiped to my profile, and handed it to Mizusawa.

Mizusawa showed that to Endo-san. "Right now, he has a little over ten thousand followers. And...yeah." Mizusawa glanced at me, and our eyes met for just an instant before he flicked his away again for some reason. "We'll double this over the next three months."

What?! I wanted to say. But then Mizusawa lightly punched at my leg, so I managed to keep myself under control. *Urk, guess he wants me to go along with it.*

"...Yes, I'll do it," I said.

"I see. That's an attractive offer," Endo-san replied.

Mizusawa gave me a scary grin, which he changed straight to a softer smile that he directed at Endo-san and Ashigaru-san. "So the details of our plan are as follows: First, nanashi uses his account to advertise the game you produce for an initial six months. And as payment, we request the production of this game. Whether or not we continue our contract after that, we'll discuss again at that time."

Having summed everything up, he finally returned the initiative he'd been holding to the other party. "How does that sound to you?"

*　*　*

"Thank you very much for today."

We were in front of the café. The discussion had concluded, we'd finished paying the check, and the five of us were standing in front of the café. By the way, since we'd been the ones to call them here, we had tried to get them to let us pay, but Ashigaru-san had told us he was going to the bathroom, and then suddenly, he'd slipped over to the register to pay. Adults sure do play dirty.

"So then, nanashi-kun, I'll be counting on you for the six months until completion," said Endo-san, repeating the deal we'd just made.

"Yes. Likewise! I'll send you the details on game specifications later," I replied.

"And he'll double his followers," Mizusawa cut in.

"Hey, you..." I shot Mizusawa a disgruntled glare for stirring things up, and Ashigaru-san and Endo-san smiled pleasantly.

Mizusawa had made his grand speech. It seemed to have convinced Endo-san—after that, based on the decision we'd discussed that he would present us with an original game in return for advertising his work for six months. Somehow, this had led to me having to increase my follower count, but well, I'd already been thinking that I had to establish a presence as a pro gamer. I should consider this just the right push in that direction.

"But anyway, Mizusawa-kun, that was amazing," Ashigaru-san said pleasantly. "That was a hell of a speech. I mean, that was the kind of presentation you'd expect from an adult."

"Oh, no." Mizusawa smiled coolly, and then a hint of sadness crossed his face. "I'm just good at saying all the right things."

It was true Mizusawa was normally good in that field, but—"saying all the right things" was a cold way to put it. It was like he was getting down on himself for still relying on "formalities."

"That was impressive when you're just in your second year of high school. Impressive enough that I'd like to work with you one day."

"Ha-ha-ha, I hope you'll take me, then, if we have the opportunity,"

Mizusawa said with his usual smile at his usual pace, exchanging words just for politeness's sake.

"Not *if there's an opportunity.*" Ashigaru-san chose to be forward.

"...Pardon?"

Ashigaru-san stuck one hand in his pocket and pulled out a black card case. He took a square piece of paper out of it and handed it to Mizusawa. "This is my card. In a few years, after you've graduated university, if you don't have other plans, then contact me any time."

"...!" Mizusawa seemed startled as he looked between Ashigaru-san and the business card he'd accepted.

Eventually, his head dropped, eyes hidden from view by his bangs. "Understood."

You could just see a little smile on his lips, as if he was coming to a realization about something.

"See you, then—my place is this way," Ashigaru-san said.

"I've got a different meeting to go to now, so," Endo-san added, and the two of them left—Ashigaru-san on foot, and Endo-san in a taxi. Things unfamiliar to me had come up constantly in that discussion, but now it was over, and the three of us were exhausted in front of the café.

"...Well, we did it. There sure has been a lot happening today," Kikuchi-san said as if letting out her earlier tension. She seemed kind of more hunched over than usual. Well, she'd been the only girl there, watching as we had kind of an adult business talk. I'd also been turned into a sort of product, so I really understood the feeling.

Well, regardless...

"That went pretty well, thanks to you, Mizusawa. I appreciate it," I said from the heart.

He popped up one eyebrow. "You're welcome. But I only accomplished that in the first place thanks to your skills, so be more proud of yourself."

"W-well...yeah... Okay." I hemmed and hawed, feeling weirdly shy at the praise.

"Hey, Fumiya," Mizusawa said in a calm tone.

"...Yeah?"

"I noticed something."

"What?" I asked back.

Mizusawa looked straight at me, as if he was trying to build me up. "Instead of trying to advertise something, you have the other person present what you want." He jabbed a finger at me.

It reminded me of that gesture of hers that I hadn't been seeing lately.

"What we're doing—it's what being a pro gamer is all about, right?"

"...Ah." Now that he said it, I thought he was totally right.

I was offering my reach, doing business, contracting with a sponsor.

And as compensation for advertising the other party during the contracted period, I would be accepting things I needed—like money or services.

This was what business looked like for Ashigaru-san and lots of other pro gamers.

"...You're right." Exhilaration steadily welled up in my chest.

It was like the feeling I got when I accomplished a difficult assignment in life strategy with Hinami.

I could move forward with this. That's what I thought. "Have I been... getting closer to my dream without even knowing it?"

And I had been guided here by none other than the shady guy who stood before me.

"Uh-huh." Mizusawa smiled boyishly.

Eventually, he opened his mouth one more time, reaffirming what we'd done today. "So this sort of thing is like..."

"Yeah?"

"Maybe it's a calling?"

"Yeah...I'm glad you'd say that." I expressed my feelings honestly, confidence inside me budding.

Then for some reason, Mizusawa said, "No, I don't just mean that." He looked somehow satisfied as he gazed out at the same old setting sun.

"Maybe this stuff...is a calling for me, too, I mean."

* * *

On the train on the way back, the three of us held on to the hanging straps as we reflected on that day.

"Now...he just has to make it, huh," said Kikuchi-san.

"Yeah." I nodded.

Mizusawa nodded, too. "Well, I did what I could. I'll let you handle the specifics now, Fumiya," he said.

"Wait, me?" I was surprised, but after a little consideration, it made sense. "But...oh yeah. I'm the one who knows Hinami the best, huh."

"Yep."

"...Yes."

There was a lot of complicated meaning in both of their remarks—but relationships are just like that to begin with. I don't think any relationship can be expressed by something as simple as a relationship chart.

"If there's anything I can do, then please let me know," Kikuchi-san said.

"I will... Thanks."

For her, it was like jealousy or guilt, or the desire to have things made clear. There was uncertainty about that chaos of feelings, atonement, and karma all jumbled together to be directed at just one person.

"If we do this, then Aoi'll be happy, too, right?" said Mizusawa.

"Yeah... I think she will be."

He felt bad because he could only live by "formalities," but he'd felt something immeasurable in someone more thoroughly committed to those formalities than him. That had turned to affection, and there lay the contradiction that generated sincere emotion.

"We know Hinami best, after all."

And then there was me—I'd always lived as an individual, but in changing myself and changing how I saw the world, I'd come to find someone who wasn't my girlfriend as uniquely special. That was my insincerity.

We probably all bore these little uncertainties, contradictions, and insincerities, occasionally pretending we didn't see them as we slowly made our way forward.

I think that might be just what life really is.

"—?!"

"Whoa, watch out, Fuka-chan."

As the train came to a sudden stop, Kikuchi-san lost her balance, swayed, and fell toward Mizusawa. He's sharp at times like that, and he caught her firmly, supporting her until she was stable.

"Th-thank you."

"It's okay. You're not hurt?"

"N-no."

Seeing Kikuchi-san looking up at Mizusawa like that, I blurted out, "H-hey! Mizusawa!"

"Hmm? What's wrong, Fumiya?"

I was letting myself get emotional. "Wh-what are you doing?"

"Huh...? She almost fell," he said.

I was surprised.

If Mizusawa hadn't caught Kikuchi-san just now, she might have fallen. He'd helped someone important to me, which meant this wasn't the reaction I should be having.

"Oh...of course." So I swallowed my emotions and said the reasonable thing. "Sorry... Thanks."

"What the heck? You're welcome." Mizusawa smiled wryly, with a teasing look on his face. "Ha-ha-ha. I've never seen you act like that before, Fumiya."

"Sh-shut up."

You can't explain everything people do with logic, I guess. Sometimes we just do weird things…s-so I'm really sorry for being rude.

* * *

Kikuchi-san and I parted ways with Mizusawa at Omiya, and I decided to walk Kikuchi-san back to her house. Mizusawa said he had something to do and went into a café at Omiya, and from there, the two of us got on the train.

We walked together along the way from Kita-Asaka Station.

"I really am glad that we worked that out… Thank you for your help, too, Kikuchi-san."

"Oh, no. I think I feel a little better now because of this… Maybe that means my motives are impure, after all…"

"That's not true."

As a creator, Kikuchi-san had overstepped with Hinami more than most people would forgive. Hinami had probably been struck by the sharpness of the lines we'd made her say during that play.

"And, um…I'm glad that you and Mizusawa get along." But even as I was saying that, remembering how I'd felt earlier didn't feel great. *No, no, it's still a good thing that they're getting along, mm-hmm.*

Kikuchi-san studied me curiously.

"Huh, wh-what?"

"Fumiya-kun…could it be…?" Her eyes peering into mine spotted my weakness. "…Were you jealous?"

"What…?! N-no, I wasn't…" I instinctively tried to put up a strong front, but it wasn't good to fixate on appearances. So I decided to take off the tough mask.

"No…that's a lie." Then I said with resignation, "You're right, I was pretty jealous."

Kikuchi-san's shoulders twitched for just an instant, and she giggled. "I'm glad. So you can get jealous, too."

"Well, I mean, I'm only human..."

For some reason, Kikuchi-san was smiling with satisfaction. "Tee-hee. I feel like this is the first time that you've been jealous since we've started dating. I'm glad."

"Th-the heck...?" I said, but I considered a little. "I-it's not like this is the first time..."

Kikuchi-san giggled devilishly. "Tee-hee. Oh, really? But I never noticed." She was still in a great mood.

"Don't be happy about it... It's hard for me."

"Is it?"

"Yeah. Especially when it's Mizusawa," I said.

Kikuchi-san blinked. "Why him?"

"W-well...because Mizusawa is that kind of guy," I said vaguely.

Kikuchi-san tilted her head, now even more blank. "You don't trust Mizusawa-kun?"

"Oh, no...that's not what I mean."

"Mm-hmm?"

"It's actually like, *because* I trust him..."

"How so?"

Maybe I wouldn't recognize this feeling in myself unless someone asked me about it. "I think that Mizusawa...and you are both really attractive people. Like, it wouldn't be strange for you two to just be drawn to each other, even if you didn't mean to go behind my back."

After staring back at me, Kikuchi-san giggled. "...You feel that strongly about me and Mizusawa-kun?"

"...Well..." I turned away while shyly scratching at my head like some manga character.

Then...

...Kikuchi-san's fingers plucked at my sleeve. "—It's all right."

She tugged me over gently.

And her lips touched mine.

"?!"

It was a light one, just a moment's touch, but it was explosive enough to blast our whole conversation out of my mind.

"You're the only one I like, Fumiya-kun," Kikuchi-san said, which sounded a lot like what I'd told her once before.

My soul had completely left my body, so the most I could do was weakly agree, "Y-yeah...me too." *Huh? Hey, she's been taking the lead for a while here...*

Eventually, the two of us reached Kikuchi-san's house.

"Thank you very much for inviting me today. I'm glad I was able to see a whole different world."

"Yeah. I should thank you for coming all this way." I nodded.

Kikuchi-san unlocked the door of her house and put her hand on it.

"Good night."

"Yeah. Night."

And so I left Kikuchi-san and walked back to Kita-Asaka Station alone, then headed home.

* * *

—Or so I thought.

"Wait...what?"

About half an hour after walking Kikuchi-san home, I got off the platform of the Saikyo Line in Omiya to change trains, where for some reason, I was meeting up with Mizusawa.

"Ha-ha-ha, don't look so suspicious."

"You told me you wanted to talk alone... Of course I'm gonna be suspicious."

"Well, I obviously couldn't stop a guy from walking his girlfriend home."

"Thanks for your concern," I said sarcastically.

"Heh-heh-heh." Mizusawa laughed. "Well, any time would've worked. But I was planning to tell you right when I decided."

"Tell me... Tell me what?" I asked, but I kind of had the feeling I knew what he was going to say.

*   *   *

"During the trip, I'm going to confess my feelings to Aoi again."

"…I see."

"Huh. You're not as surprised as I thought you'd be."

I hadn't guessed exactly what he was planning to tell me. But… "Well, it's you, so you'd be doing something I wouldn't expect. So this is just what I expected."

"Ha-ha-ha. So you saw it coming?"

Then a sad smile crossed his face. "But this is just a confession. It's not like I've made any progress since summer vacation, and I know it's not gonna happen." Then he seemed to remember something. "We were talking about it recently, right? How it's unusual for her to show her exhaustion like that."

"Yeah."

"And from what I've heard, it's probably because of you, right?"

"That's not…" I started to deny it, but Mizusawa gave me a look.

"…True?" His remark was short but punchy, and there was a sharp glint in his eye. I was speechless.

He was actually right. I was probably the one to get closest to her real feelings, ever since she'd first put on her mask.

That's why I opened my mouth again to swallow the words I'd just said. "No…I have wondered if it does maybe have something to do with me."

"Yeah, huh." Then Mizusawa pierced me with a powerful and aggressive look. "I hate to put it like this—but this is an opportunity."

"…An opportunity?"

"Aoi's mask is so thick that even if I'm really open with her, she'd just turn it back on me and run off. But—it seems like she's weak right now." Mizusawa raised a silly eyebrow. "That never happens, right?"

"What the heck? You're playing dirty."

"Ha-ha-ha. I'm fine with that. You know what I'm like." Then his smile melted away again. "But that's not what I really mean when I say 'opportunity.'" He grinned provocatively.

"—It's that my number one rival for Aoi's affections is another girl."

"!"

He didn't have to say who he meant.

"I'm not the type to hold on too tight to anything. I feel like whatever happens, happens, but…" You could take that as a proclamation or a declaration of war. "I've decided that when I want something, I'll do everything I can to reach out for it. So, Fumiya…" Something about the way he said my name made this feel strangely real.

"—Let's make this surprise a success."

4

A boss that won't take damage no matter what you do is often weak to healing

A few weeks later, the nineteenth of March arrived on a Saturday. It was Aoi Hinami's birthday—and the day of the trip.

What Mizusawa had said had been spinning around in my head this whole time.

"During the trip, I'm going to confess my feelings to Aoi again."

It wasn't like that was bad news for me.

I mean, I was dating Kikuchi-san, and I trusted Mizusawa as a person. I could even say that I trusted him the most of the guys.

So if he was right about confessing his feelings now, when Hinami was more vulnerable, and the two of them started dating, then I would have no objections—in fact, I'd even welcome it.

"But…what is this feeling…?"

It probably wasn't jealousy. I wasn't in love with her.

But for some reason, I had complicated feelings about Aoi Hinami getting into a romantic relationship with someone.

"This is complicated… This is life…"

I was still unable to put it into words as I got ready to go. In my bag was the minimum change of clothing, plus a board game to enjoy with everyone. I also had the tablet where I'd saved the data Ashigaru-san had sent me the day before.

This was our present for Hinami—and we hadn't just left it all to

Ashigaru-san. We'd also packed in what we could manage for this original game for her.

I figured we could make her happy with this. Even if it didn't quite reach her heart, maybe it could just barely touch it. I wanted this to push me into sitting down and really considering my and Hinami's relationship.

What I should be doing here wasn't forcing anything on her or prying into her business, but talking with her.

My notebook had been open on the table since the day before. With a glance, I checked what was written in it.

It was the "assignment" that I'd given myself for this trip.

"Talk with Hinami about how we really feel."

I checked the LINE chat that I'd sent Hinami about a week ago. Displayed there was the message I'd sent—[*During the trip next week, I want to talk with you alone at some point*].

There was no response, but there was a "read" notification. She hadn't blocked me. So then could I assume I had some hope?

"I'm going now."

No one else was awake yet that weekend, so I made my stealthy farewell to the quiet house and walked out to the station.

* * *

When I arrived at Kitayono Station, I thought back on the camping trip that summer.

Oh yeah, didn't I walk to our meeting spot with Mimimi that time?

I think back then, we'd trusted each other as friends and comrades in arms, but we hadn't been thinking of each other that way. That was why we'd been able to make the trip together.

Mimimi had expressed her thanks to me and told me that I was her hero and stuff, reinvigorating my enthusiasm for taking life seriously. I thought we'd gotten closer from that, but now we were going to Omiya separately.

"The local train bound for Omiya is now arriving."

The station announcements were very familiar to me after living here for so many years. When I heard it, I stepped aboard.

A year ago, I'd only ever taken this train to go to school alone, buy video games alone, and go to the arcade alone, but suddenly, I was going with Hinami to buy clothing or having her take me to go shopping with the others. Thanks to her, I'd spent less and less time on my own.

And then before you know it, even without her, I was using this train for so many things—going on dates with Kikuchi-san or heading to my part-time job, where Mizusawa was.

As the townscape of Saitama flowed by out the window, I wistfully remembered the time that wouldn't return.

"Nothing here is any different," I whispered to myself on the nigh-empty train—it was close to the first one of the morning.

The cityscape, the light shining in, the swaying of the train.

None of it had changed since then.

But everything had changed about the view I saw. It had to be me who had changed.

And it went without saying that the one who'd pushed me to change was Hinami.

Eventually, the train arrived in Omiya. I got off and went down the steps from the platform of the Saikyo Line, then headed for the platform for lines one and two.

The girl I'd chosen was sitting on a seat on the platform around the area of car four.

"…Good morning."

"Yeah, morning."

Once Kikuchi-san and I had met up on the station platform, we got on the train headed for Shinagawa.

* * *

"Oh yeah...so why the uniform?" I asked Kikuchi-san.

"Oh, yes, that!"

We were on the train on the Keihin-Tohoku Line. Even though it was a holiday and we were all about to go to USJ, for some reason, Kikuchi-san was wearing the Sekitomo High School uniform.

"Actually...I was talking about things with the other girls, and we were saying we wanted to do USJ-niforms!" Kikuchi-san said in a bubbly tone.

"Ohhh," I replied brightly.

USJ-niform is a normie word. As the term implies, it means to go to USJ wearing your school uniform. It's that thing where high school girls upload their glamorous adventures on Instagram or TikTok or whatever. It's a very new experience to hear that kind of influencer lingo come out of Kikuchi-san's mouth, but I'm a fan of seeing her play the classic high school girl.

"This is a first for me, and I'm looking forward to it!" Kikuchi-san said, sounding unusually cheery and enthused.

I smiled at her. "Ah-ha-ha, I really get that."

Kikuchi-san was shyly startled, blushing. "O-oh, really?"

"Yeah. I'm glad to know you're gonna have a good time."

"Tee-hee. I really can't wait. What about you, Tomozaki-kun?" she asked.

"I'm really looking forward to it, too. This is my first time going to an amusement park with friends...," I said, then immediately wondered if I was sharing something too negative.

But Kikuchi-san seemed happy about that fact. "O-oh, yes! Me too!" she said. So that was okay.

"Yeah. And also..." Trying to hide my growing shyness, I said, "It's also my first time going on a trip with my girlfriend...so I'm looking forward to that, too."

"Oh..."

Now I was getting embarrassed. "Oh, well, ha-ha, you know," I said in attempt to cover it up. I'm weak.

"Tomozaki-kun!"

"Hmm?"

The smile on her face didn't belong to an angel or a fairy—just a sweet girl. "—Let's have lots of fun!"

"Yeah... For sure!"

Under the light of her sunny expression, I couldn't help but smile.

If my goal and what Mizusawa had declared to me were actually going to happen—then this trip was bound to change something about our relationships.

So I would enjoy the coming time as much as I could.

That's what I was thinking.

* * *

About an hour after that.

I was near the ticket gates of the boarding area of the Shinagawa Station Shinkansen.

Hinami, Mizusawa, Nakamura, and Tama-chan had arrived at the meetup spot ahead of time. By the way, though Hinami and Tama-chan were both wearing uniforms, they weren't quite according to the dress code. *Now this is looking like USJ-niforms.* Meanwhile, the guys were in regular clothes.

"Oh! You guys are here!" Hinami called out to me lightly.

"Morning... Man, I'm tired," I muttered to no one in particular.

"Morning. Looking forward to it so much you couldn't sleep?" Hinami said, her mask remaining fully on.

"...Yeah." I was a little curt. Maybe she felt something was off from my gloomy tone of voice. But I still couldn't bring myself to engage with her in communication made up of nothing but formalities.

Looking around the area, I opened my mouth to change the topic. "Umm, so now it's just Mimimi, Izumi, and Takei, huh?" When I listed out the names of those who weren't here yet, it felt very right. The three of them would have a hard time getting out of bed. If I had to say, I probably would have guessed that Takei would wake up and get here first from sheer excitement, but apparently this time, the needle had swung around to sleeping in.

"About that, Fumiya. If you're looking for Takei, he's over there," Mizusawa said pleasantly as he pointed to the ticket gate for the Shinkansen boarding area.

"Huh?"

There, on the other side of the ticket gate, was Takei, watching us with dewy eyes. For some reason, he was the only one of the guys wearing his uniform. Guess he wanted to do the USJ-niform thing, too.

"Wahhhhh! Don't leave me all aloooone!"

"We'll get everyone together before we go. Just wait there," Nakamura said with a scowl.

Beside him, Mizusawa was chuckling. "Heh-heh-heh. Apparently, he was so excited that he got here first and even went into the Shinkansen ticket gates."

"Well, that's a relief." If that's what happened, that really made sense.

"How so?"

"I was right about Takei."

"Huh?"

Right then, Mimimi and Izumi arrived at almost the same time.

"Sorry to make you waaaait!"

When I glanced at the clock, it was exactly six. On time according to the minute hand, not so much according to the second hand. It was very them.

"All right, we're all here. Has everyone bought drinks and stuff?" Hinami was already taking charge.

"I bought mine at the convenience store on the way!" Mimimi replied, and the others nodded.

"All right! Then let's get going!" Hinami said cheerily, and with her in the lead, we went through the Shinkansen ticket gates.

"Ohhhhhh! I was so looooonely! Guyyyyyys!"

Though it hadn't even been a minute since the trip had begun, Takei was yelling like we were having an emotional reunion. Ignoring him, we headed to the Shinkansen boarding area.

* * *

"Around here?" Mizusawa said as he looked at the numbers on the tickets. We'd gotten them for everyone beforehand, and now we were getting onto the Shinkansen to head to Osaka. Then we'd drop off our bags at the accommodations and go straight to USJ.

"Hey, hey! What are we doing about seats?!" Izumi asked excitedly.

"Oh, those are written on the tickets. But as long as it's the nine of us in these seats, we can each take whichever one, right?"

"O-oh, of course…!" Kikuchi-san said. It was unusual for her to speak up, but I could understand why she'd want to right then.

We'd gotten all these seats at once, and they'd been issued all at once. We'd just handed them out to everyone that morning without much consideration as to who would be beside who. If we sat down according to the numbers we'd just been handed, then Kikuchi-san might be sitting far from me and feel awkward. And Tama-chan could be beside Takei. That was the one thing we had to avoid.

But then I recalled the assignment I'd given myself.

The trip was still long, but wouldn't this be my first big chance to talk alone with Hinami? Of course, I didn't know how deep a conversation we could have out where anyone could hear. But we had two hours until we arrived in Osaka, so maybe I could make some kind of progress.

That's why I decided to take the lead in the conversation and try making the proposal myself. "Umm, what numbers do the seats cover?"

"8D, and 9 to 12 of D and E."

Basically, we'd secured four rows of seats in pairs, and one seat in front of that. Only the one at the head was a solo seat.

"Let's sit wherever we want in that area and not worry about which numbers we have," I said.

"Oh, yes! Let's do that!" Kikuchi-san said with a firm nod and distinct relief.

Her reaction made me hesitate. *Hmm, maybe I should take the initiative and invite her to sit next to me.*

So I was thinking, when—

"Fuka-chan! Sit with me!" Izumi pointed at Kikuchi-san.

"M-me?"

"Yeah! You don't want to?"

"N-no, I do! L-let's do it!"

"Yay! Oh, who'll take the window?"

And so the two of them briskly took some nearby seats. For a moment, I wondered what was going on here, but after a little thought, I thought I knew.

Izumi was probably being considerate.

Maybe it would ease Kikuchi-san's fears if I took the initiative here and asked her to sit with me, but if I'd taken too long, then she might have wound up on her own. I think Izumi had considered that possibility and approached her first. I was glad of that, but it also meant she hadn't trusted me to take care of Kikuchi-san. I was grateful, but sad.

On the other hand, I didn't have to worry anymore. I could sit with anyone now.

Then we got stuck.

I looked around to see Mimimi and Tama-chan were giving each other eye signals.

If you thought about it, there were five girls here: Hinami, Mimimi, Tama-chan, Izumi, and Kikuchi-san. Kikuchi-san and Izumi forming a pair just now made three left.

There were also four boys: me, Nakamura, Mizusawa, and Takei. If we made two pairs of boys, then one of the girls would wind up alone. Hinami's birthday was the main event that day, so that one shouldn't be Hinami.

Whoever was left out of the pair made next would be in the lone seat— that made it a little difficult for anyone to make the next invitation.

So I made up my mind.

If someone would be left over no matter what and I wanted to talk to Hinami, then I should—

"Hey Aoi, let's sit here."

His gentle voice slid naturally into the atmosphere.

"Oh? What's up, Takahiro?" Hinami replied with indomitable spirit. Mizusawa gave her a cool smile back. "What d'you mean? Is something strange?"

That's right—Mizusawa was the one who called her name.

"...No, not really."

"Then sit next to me. You can take the window seat. Just send me the photos after."

"Ah-ha-ha. You're always so nice."

This turn of events struck Kikuchi-san and me, at least. Izumi was also sensitive to this stuff, leaping up to stare at the two of them. She loved romantic gossip, so maybe she'd picked up on Mizusawa's feelings. Or maybe she was just a curious onlooker reading in too deeply.

Well, the point of this trip was to show Hinami a good time, so of course we couldn't leave her alone. This wasn't a very strange thing to do. But—

"During the trip, I'm going to confess my feelings to Aoi again."

I remembered what Mizusawa had said that night in Omiya.

I knew enough to guess Mizusawa wasn't doing this to keep Hinami from being left alone—

Then something hit me. I'd given myself the goal during this trip of talking with Hinami about how we really felt. But Mizusawa was also planning to get closer to her during this trip and confess his feelings to her.

I did want to support Mizusawa, after all, so it was fine that he was taking the initiative to talk to her...but that meant that I'd have fewer chances for my own conversation. And the reverse was also true.

Meaning over following two days, my greatest rival would be—

"Aoi, is that sweater a new one from this year?"

"Oh! You always notice the details, Takahiro."

—the guy who had just very slickly nabbed Hinami.

"...For real?"

With a rival this capable, I was in trouble. He can be a reassuring ally, but having him on the other side bumps up the difficulty level too high. Couldn't we form a united front?

"So then..." A low and grumpy voice reached my ears. I was pulled out of my thoughts and back to the situation at hand. That voice was Nakamura's.

I looked over to see Mimimi and Tama-chan were already sitting together as an obvious set, while me, Nakamura, and Takei were left over. Meaning one of us would be sitting alone. Well, I wouldn't have a problem being temporarily alone; I mean, that's nothing to me, but having someone to talk to would make the trip more enjoyable.

And then—Nakamura.

"...Tomozaki, sit with me."

"S-sure." I sat down beside Nakamura. *Umm...oh, wow.*

"Sh-Shujiiii?"

And with that sorrowful cry from Takei, I found out that in Nakamura's list of "people I want to sit beside," at the very least, I beat out Takei.

* * *

It was a few minutes after the Shinkansen set off.

"..."

"..."

Silence flowed between me and Nakamura.

I wanted to complain like, *Hey, you're the one who picked me, so make it less awkward*, but I couldn't think of anything in particular to say, either, so I couldn't criticize. Nakamura and I don't really have much in common, so even if we were supposed to suddenly start talking, I couldn't quite think of anything to say. We were both the type to always say what we mean. If there was nothing we really wanted to ask or say, we'd just remain silent.

"—Right?!"

The chatter from the seats ahead of us came to my ears. Each pair formed when deciding seats had just taken whichever was closest, meaning Mimimi and Tama-chan were sitting in front of us. By the way, Izumi and Kikuchi-san were behind us, and in front of Mimimi and Tama-chan was Hinami and Mizusawa, and Takei was all alone at the head.

Then my attention was drawn to one point—the seats two rows in front of me—where Mizusawa and Hinami were sitting.

"..."

Instantly, the quiet went to silence for the sake of listening to their conversation. It did kind of feel like eavesdropping, but after hearing Mizusawa's declaration of his feelings, it would be impossible not to pay attention to their conversation. And it wasn't like I was trying to listen while they were alone in a room together, so I wasn't committing any crimes. This was legal, okay?

Having finished a perfect rationalization, I fixed my attention on Mizusawa and Hinami. Thanks to that cocktail party effect or whatever it's called, if I focused on them, I should be able to hear what they were talking about.

* * *

"—Right?!"

"…yeah, right?!"

"…totally is, right?!"

But Takei, sitting in front of them, kept trying to cut into Mimimi and Tama-chan's conversation, and he was so loud, all I could hear was his voice. I furrowed my brow and sighed.

"What's up with you? …If you feel sick, don't puke on me."

I must have looked awful, as Nakamura was suspecting something else entirely.

"Oh, no, I'm fine…"

I quickly gave up on trying to listen in.

* * *

It was about half an hour after the Shinkansen's departure. Nakamura was in the window seat leaning his cheek on his hand, apparently bored as he watched the scenery, when he suddenly opened his mouth. "So that reminds me."

By the way, Nakamura had dropped into the window seat without really saying anything, leaving me sitting on the aisle side before I could blink. Not that I have a strong preference, but most people think the window is better. Considering how things were between the two of us, I didn't like him taking it without even asking. I'd take the window seat without a word on the way back.

"Yeah?"

"What did you decide on for the surprise?" he asked me.

"Oh…" I glanced at Hinami's seat ahead. I didn't want her to hear, but I still couldn't hear what they were saying, even if I listened for it, so it probably went both ways.

"Well, you know…it's video game related."

"Ahh, I figured."

"You did?" I asked.

Nakamura's expression didn't change much as he continued, "I mean, you know a lot about that side of Aoi. So we made sure not to do the same thing."

"You did...?" That remark made me a little curious. "What did you guys do?"

"Oh...well, it's some emotional type of thing."

"What does that mean?" I asked back blankly.

But Nakamura wouldn't tell me any more than that. "We left most of it to Yuzu. She really loves that stuff."

"True... She'd be into planning that." Considering how she'd talked about repaying us for the camp, it seemed she felt more strongly about this than the others.

We were going to give her a pretty involved present, too, with this original video game, but maybe Izumi would prove a powerful rival in the Make Hinami Happy Championship.

"It seems like you guys would be pretty into it, too, though. Especially Takahiro." Nakamura suddenly brought up Mizusawa.

"Huh? Um...y-yeah." Now that Mizusawa had made his declaration, it was really hard for me to answer that. Exactly how did he mean that? "What do you mean, 'especially Mizusawa'?" I answered, playing innocent.

Nakamura's eyebrows scrunched down. "I mean, 'cause he likes Aoi a lot."

That surprised me. Everyone knew Nakamura was dense, so if he'd noticed, then it must be pretty obvious. Well, Mizusawa had casually mentioned it to Kikuchi-san and Ashigaru-san, so I guess that meant he wasn't going to hide it.

"Ahh...yeah, that's true."

"Huhh, so you've noticed, too? Not bad," Nakamura said with pride.

The only response I could manage was a noise. "O-oh, uh-huh." I wanted to fire a comeback at him, like *What makes you think you'd notice before me?* But I was sitting right next to him; there was no escape from here. On this playing field, his physical strength gave him the overwhelming advantage. So I swallowed that remark back down.

"It's kind of a relief."

Now that was an interesting thing for him to say. "It is?"

"He's kinda, like...not really interested in people."

"Ohh..."

I could kind of get that. Well, he'd gained an interest in me for some reason, ever since the incident where I'd told off Erika Konno. He thought I was kinda funny, like a shoujo manga heroine. But you could kind of tell that Mizusawa was fundamentally disinterested in the people around him.

The people Mizusawa was interested in were always different from "normal"—either me or Hinami, or lately, Ashigaru-san.

"Like when I was in a fight over family stuff, if I didn't talk about it, Takahiro would always stay out of it and just watch."

"Oh yeah. I get that."

It was kind of similar to my individualist mindset. Even if someone was in trouble, Mizusawa wouldn't get involved unless they asked for help. Though on that point, I believe that I have no *right* to be involved, so it's a little different.

"Takei gets overenthusiastic with his concern. He'll be like, *Shuji! C'mon, you can count on me!* Does he even know how to tone it down?"

"Ha-ha-ha. You're total opposites, huh. I mean like, coolheaded vs hotblooded." So in a sense, Nakamura might actually be the one balancing out this group.

"...But why is it a relief for you?" I asked, curious.

That reminded me: I'd spoken alone with Mizusawa, and we'd shared things openly that we couldn't say to others, but...I didn't know how other people saw Mizusawa.

After thinking a bit, still turned the other way, Nakamura spoke again. "He's generally unemotional. Good at working things out with everyone. He doesn't really put forth his own ideas about what he wants to do."

"Yeah, he knows how to get along." I nodded.

"That's why he can get along with someone strong-willed like me."

"You're self-aware of that...?" It seemed the king knew himself better than I thought. It'd be nice if he acted on it a little more, then.

"But with Aoi, he's kind of overeager. I feel like he's letting his guard down now."

I could really understand what he was talking about.

Ever since the camp that summer, Mizusawa had been having doubts about formalities and being cool—he was struggling to get away from those things. And if even dense Nakamura had picked up on this, then the results really had to be showing in his behavior.

"Lately, Takahiro has been going along with me less and less. He really pushes for the places where he wants to go hang out, and sometimes, he'll be like, 'There's something I wanna do' and cancels at the last minute... He just did that last Sunday."

"...Last Sunday..." While I totally knew what Mizusawa had been doing that Sunday, it seemed best not to touch on it for my own safety. I pulled out the insincere "Ha-ha-ha" I'd learned from Mizusawa.

Of course, Nakamura didn't notice that. He took full advantage of the privilege of the window seat, lips curving upward just slightly as he watched the scenery fly by.

"Well, sometimes, it can get to be a hassle—but I know he enjoys it that way."

* * *

And so we spent two hours on the Shinkansen to arrive at Shin-Osaka Station.

The moment we got off the Shinkansen, Mimimi loudly announced in a fake Kansai accent, "Tamaaa! How's business, darlin'?!"

"You're already talking like an Osakan!" Tama-chan jabbed back at her. Their banter was the same as always, even in another city. While they chatted, my eyes swept over the platform where we'd disembarked.

I wouldn't say it was so much different from what you'd see in Saitama or Tokyo, unless you really studied the details. I didn't really feel like I'd moved very far across the familiar map of Japan, and yet here we were in Osaka. What a strange feeling.

"Wow! It really says Osaka!" Izumi was weirdly excited by the station sign.

"Yeah, duh," Nakamura shot back.

"This is my first time coming to Osaka, you know," Hinami said in a rather bouncy tone.

"Really?" Mizusawa replied. "Huh, that's surprising."

Their conversation was casual—it was probably catching my attention because I was hyperaware of them. But I feel like there's no helping it after the stuff I'd heard before.

Soon after, Kikuchi-san's mouth was also opening in awe. "W-wow. It's Osaka."

"Is this your first time, Kikuchi-san?" I asked her.

"Y-yes. What about you, Tomozaki-kun?"

"I've apparently come a long time ago, with my family."

"...Apparently?"

"Yeah. It was when I was in kindergarten, so I don't really remember. So this is basically my first time."

"Tee-hee, then we're the same."

"Ah-ha-ha, right?"

Walking along as I learned that Kikuchi-san apparently liked to share firsts, I realized that the two of us had fallen behind everyone else.

"Oh, they're getting ahead of us," she said.

"Yeah."

Right now, it kind of felt like I was on a trip with just Kikuchi-san. It got my heart pounding a little. Maybe that wasn't good when this was supposed to be a group trip, but I found myself wanting this moment to last as long as possible.

"Whoa! Look at that, Farm Boy! They really do stand on the right side!" Takei called out loud to us, ruining the mood.

Ha-ha-ha, you blockhead. Takei always has the worst timing.

But when I looked in the direction Takei pointed, everyone really was standing on the right side of the escalator. "Oh...? It's true! You're right!" I cried out.

It was that thing where they stand on the left side in eastern Japan, and the right in western Japan. I'm the type to get a little excited about slightly weird stuff like that, so I shared Takei's excitement. It was like we're on the same level, frustratingly. But it *is* kinda weird.

"It's cool, huh?!" Takei gushed.

"Yeah, I wonder how that happened when we're all Japanese...," I said.

Then I snapped out of our conversation with a start, turning around to see Kikuchi-san was watching the two of us with a pleasant smile. *That's a relief.*

"Hiro! Where should we go from here?" Izumi asked Mizusawa like she was lost.

"Well, the hotel is a short ways away from Unlimited City Station... We can drop our bags off before check-in time, so that comes first."

"Roger that! Is that like Maihama Station?"

"Uh-huh, yeah, yeah." Mizusawa agreed, almost like he was shrugging her off.

"Okay! I'll look it up!" Izumi diverted all her attention toward her phone. It was like Mizusawa was the advisor and Izumi was the worker.

"It says it's the...Tokaido Sanyo? Main line! ...Huh?! You get there in ten minutes from Osaka Station?! That's even more convenient than Maihama!"

Izumi must have really loved the Tokyo land of dreams. She based everything on a Maihama standard, and she was surprised at how close USJ was to the city center. Looking it up myself, I was surprised, too. USJ was about five stations away from Osaka Station. That's super convenient—Maihama should try a little harder. It takes about an hour to get there from Omiya.

"Umm, it says platform seven!"

"Right… Um, platform seven…," Mizusawa said as he looked around the area.

I see, maybe this is my moment. "Mimimi!" I called.

"What's up, Brain?"

"Which one is platform seven?"

"Huh? Um…I think it's this one! Left!"

"Thanks. Mizusawa, it's right."

"Roger."

"Hey!"

I used Mimimi's awful sense of direction to our benefit, and we headed to Unlimited City Station. And yes, it really was the one to the right. Just what you'd expect of Mimimi. You can trust her.

* * *

"Ooooh!"

And so we arrived at Unlimited City Station.

When we came out of the ticket gates, we were suddenly welcomed by a giant dinosaur sign, and it got us really excited, even though we weren't in the park yet. The station area was overflowing with tourists despite the early hour—I guess that's what you'd expect from the largest theme park in the Kansai region.

"It's right there in front of us, but we still can't go yet… Agh, so tantalizing!" Mimimi was practically vibrating with impatience.

But since we were all walking around with large backpacks or wheeled luggage, we couldn't go straight to USJ. So first, we headed to the hotel to drop off our bags.

"So you booked the hotel, right, Yuzu?" Mizusawa asked.

Izumi nodded. "Yeah. Unsurprisingly, a weekend stay at the official hotel right by the park was too expensive for us…," she said with a thousand-yard stare.

"A realistic choice, then! Well done!" Mimimi said with a salute.

*　*　*

We walked for about ten minutes, then arrived at a hotel that was close to USJ.

"Ohhh! So this is what it's like!" Tama-chan said, and Mimimi nodded. The place was less a hotel and more a fancy housing-complex sort of building. Kind of like a guesthouse, where foreigners stay.

The first floor was a large shared space, which split off into separate dormitory rooms. By the way, I'd heard that when we told them during booking that we had a birthday girl, they said they'd lend us this space for the night. Local hospitality, I guess.

"Thank you for handling these!"

We went in through the entrance and dropped off our large luggage at the front desk. Izumi had booked four rooms that could accommodate two to three people, and we had nine. The guys would stay in two pairs, while the girls would be two and three.

We naturally split the rooms so that we could talk about the surprise—we went with me and Mizusawa, Nakamura and Takei, the Mimi-Tama duo, and then Hinami, Kikuchi-san, and Yuzu as a trio.

We dropped off our bags room by room. Us guys dropped off our bags first and waited outside.

After a while, we could hear Mimimi's cheery voice. "Ta-daaaa!"

The glass doors opened to reveal Mimimi in a green cap and Izumi with the headband of a colorful American character. They must have bought them beforehand. I was impressed at how prepared they were.

"If you're going to USJ, you've gotta wear these!" Izumi declared.

"Absolutely!" Mimimi agreed.

"She's right!" Hinami followed up with enthusiasm.

Tama-chan, however, was looking like she'd been dragged into this unwillingly. "Hmm, sure, I guess..." She was wearing a hat that matched Mimimi's. Tama-chan already was small like a woodland creature, so it really suited her.

Hinami wore the same hat that Mimimi and Tama-chan had, but in red. The "main character" look, basically. *Well, she is the star of this trip, after all.*

Then my eyes sought out a certain girl.

If these four were wearing hats, then that meant—

"...Umm, this is a little embarrassing." That clear voice led me to the girl I was looking for—a fairy wearing a headband that matched Izumi's.

An "oh" of almost-wonder slipped out of me as my eyes met with Kikuchi-san's. Her face was bright red. Then we both got shy and looked away from each other.

There was a spurt of laughter from the side.

"...What?" I demanded.

The source of that laughter was Nakamura, who was smirking at us. "You guys are so blushy."

"...Shaddap." I mean, no matter how many dates we'd been on, she's still so cute. In fact, I think I deserve some praise for holding on to this feeling.

"Um...it suits you."

"Th-thank you...!"

"Hey, stop flirting!" Tama-chan snapped.

With that, we finally headed off to USJ.

* * *

"Here we are!" Mimimi struck a pose with the utmost excitement. After leaving behind our bags, we were ready and returned to Unlimited City Station.

"This is amazing, huh. It's like we're already in USJ," Hinami said as she looked all around.

She was right—it was a few minutes' more walk to the USJ entrance, but stroll along here, and you'd find a sign with a famous movie gorilla climbing a high-rise, the open door of a shop that sold USJ merch, and a Western-style pizza chain that was uncommon elsewhere. But then suddenly, there were also normal chain stores like McDonald's and MOS Burger, which made the place feel multinational. The townscape had the pop atmosphere of a Hollywood movie mixed with the vibe of modern video games and anime. We were getting excited about the park now.

"What should I do now?! Maybe I should go to the bathroom?!" Izumi found the strangest thing to be worried about.

"Uh, it's not like there's no bathrooms inside," Nakamura shot back coolly.

"Oh! Really?!"

The two of them really created an amazing balance.

"G-guys! Look!" Izumi called out in awe.

When we reached the gates, that USJ thing that everyone knows popped into view.

It was a large globe that slowly rotated around, with a spray of water spurting out into the blue sky of March in the background. The word *Unlimited* was wrapped around it. It was the globe that you've probably seen a hundred times in videos and stuff, looming right above us.

"Ohh! This is it! It's literally the planet Earth!" Takei cried out, which was a very Takei thing to say.

"It's literally not, though," I shot back at him, though I was a little awed myself. Seeing it in real life, it felt so three-dimensional—it has a real presence. I get why he said that.

"Hey, guys! Let's take a photo!" Mimimi proposed.

"Yeah! I've been wanting to take a photo here!" Izumi jumped on that idea, and they dragged us all into a line in front of it. I'm not normally much of a picture-taker, but even I wanted to take a photo in front of this globe. It's similar to the desire to unlock a well-known achievement.

"Thank you very much! Here, please!"

Then with Mimimi's inborn communication skills, she swiftly found someone to take a photo for us, and we slid right into a photo shoot.

"Of course, Aoi is right in the middle!" Izumi prodded the star of the day right in there.

"Ah-ha-ha, okay, okay." Though Hinami made a face, she seemed to be enjoying herself.

"Okay, cheese."

""""Hexactly!"""" we all called out at once.

And then with all of us wrapped around Hinami, we took the cliché tourist photo in front of the giant globe by the entrance gates. Well, it's like Mimimi often says—the cliché is the most beautiful. I've come to understand quite a bit about life.

* * *

"Thank you very much!"

We were at the ticket window at the entrance, using our phones to give the numbers for the tickets we'd reserved and receive all our physical tickets.

And now it was time for Hinami's first surprise.

After accepting the tickets, Mimimi clapped a hand on Hinami's shoulder and said to the front desk, "Miss! It's her birthday today!"

"Ohh! Happy birthdaaay!"

"Ah-ha-ha, thank you." Hinami thanked the staff, though she seemed a little bewildered.

"Since it's your birthday today, please put this somewhere that will stand out as you explore the park!" And then she handed to Mimimi a sticker shaped like a yellow badge that had *"Happy Birthday"* written on it.

"Huh?"

"All right, aaaand equip!" Mimimi stuck the yellow, attention-getting sticker on Hinami's chest.

There's a sticker at USJ that they only give to people who say it's their birthday, and it gets you special treatment at some places in the park.

"Oh…is that what this is?" Hinami must have figured it out, as she accepted it with resignation. But she already stood out because of her good looks, and now this.

It wasn't in her character, but Hinami reacted playfully to it. "This is a little embarrassing, isn't it?" she said, and we all laughed together.

But I had complicated feelings about her performativity, and I'm sure Kikuchi-san and Mizusawa did, too. I'm sure Hinami wouldn't be moved by mere formalities—she'd come to expect those.

Right as I was thinking that, Mimimi said to the lady at the front desk, "Ma'am! Could we have another five of these?!"

"Sure! Absolutely!"

"Huh?"

Hinami didn't get what was going on, and neither did anyone else, myself included. But Mimimi took those five stickers, and—

"All riiiight! No blind spots!"

—Mimimi stuck them onto Hinami's right and left shoulder, plus one on her back and two on her skirt, so they clearly stood out.

"Now you're the birthday girl from every angle! Perfect!"

"Hey, Mimimi, is this really necessary?"

Hinami was already wearing a school uniform and an attention-getting red hat. Now she had six stickers, and suddenly, she was the queen of USJ. It was a dramatic contrast from her usual. Even I found it a little funny.

Hinami checked out her reflection in the little mirror by the reception window and discovered how silly Mimimi had made her look. Though she seemed a little disgruntled, she had a crooked smile on.

That was when some staff who had been cleaning saw Hinami's stickers and called out to her, "Ah! Happy birthday!" Kicked while she was down.

"Ah-ha-ha! Thank you!" Hinami chirped back. Despite the bewildering barrage of stickers, of course she quickly adapted to the situation.

"Hey, that lady got stickers! I want one, too!"

"Hmm? Oh, you only get those if it's your birthday, Yoshi-kun."

"Oh, really?! Heyyyy! Happy birthdaaay!"

Though Hinami was surprised to be caught by such an innocent congratulations, she replied, "Ah-ha-ha...yeah, thanks!" I don't know how much of that reaction was sincere, but I think she was real just for a moment there. Hinami struggles the most to deal with situations where people pull her into things she can't control.

"Geez...already?" she griped.

"Heh-heh-heh! We haven't even gotten to the main event, Aoi!" Mimimi cackled.

"Yes, yes, I'm looking forward to it."

And so Aoi Hinami's birthday party began. Was Hinami happy about this christening, or was she just taking it as a fact?

I didn't know what she felt in the real sense, so I didn't know. At the very least, I was going to sincerely enjoy and sincerely celebrate Hinami's special day. It was simple, but important.

* * *

We went through luggage inspection and the ticket check and finally entered USJ.

"Ohh..."

As soon as we entered, we were greeted by an old-fashioned American scene. Tall, slim coconut trees grew at fixed intervals in front of rows of Western-style buildings, the dark green of the leaves and blue of the sky vivid to the eye. Fancy cinematic music was playing from every direction; it felt like a foreign town where a little festival was being held. Even the decorative signs read STOP in English. It was kinda fun, and just being there got me excited.

However...

"Guys, follow me!" Izumi called.

...there wasn't time to bask in the atmosphere, and we just followed after Izumi.

"Don't run! But walk as fast as you can!" She gave incredibly particular directions as she walked in the lead, expression utterly serious.

They say that the most vital moment is right after the park opens—that's what decides your fate: whether you can get on the popular attractions quickly or not. Apparently, Izumi had actually researched how to tour the park efficiently. She's real serious about USJ.

By the way, since Hinami's presence loudly proclaimed it was her birthday, staff called "Happy birthday!" out to her multiple times as we walked past.

Yes, congratulate her even more!

"Yuzu, where are we going first?" Nakamura asked Izumi.

"Hollywood Fire Fright! The backdrop one!"

"Huh."

As I was listening to their conversation from the side, I felt a tap low on my arm. When I turned around, there was Tama-chan, walking at a quick pace. Since her strides were shorter, she was working quite a bit harder than the rest of us to keep up.

"Tomozaki, do you know what that is?" she asked.

"Umm…I think…"

My gamer spirit knows that forewarned is forearmed when you go to USJ, so I'd looked up the attractions and the food. And according to my information, the attraction Izumi had just mentioned—

"That's the one that's different—it runs backward. Plus, it shakes you around in every direction. People say it's one of the scariest at USJ."

"Oh, really? Looking forward to it," Tama-chan replied without a lot of emotion. She didn't seem like she was very scared. And this was Tama-chan, who never lied, so that meant she wasn't just putting on a strong front. She just wasn't really scared of roller coasters. It seemed like she was thinking, *Well, if it doesn't kill me, I'm fine.*

By the way, since I had no memory of having gone to an amusement park since middle school, I didn't really know if I can handle the scream machines or not. But well, I do kind of think that it's fine, since it doesn't kill you.

"I-I'm scared, too…but it's the most popular, so if we miss our chance now, then the wait'll be really long!" Despite her fear, Izumi seemed positive about it.

But for some reason, Nakamura was the opposite. "Hmm...so if that happens, shouldn't we just go on some other ride?"

"After coming all this way, we've gotta ride the most popular one!"

"Well...you could argue that, I guess...," Nakamura muttered, although he sounded unsure.

...Hold on...does this mean...?

"...Nakamura, are you scared of roller coasters?" I said.

Nakamura glared at me, and his clenched fist came for my shoulder.

But I wouldn't get hit by the same punch twice—although, technically speaking, I've been hit a bunch of times. Well, I wasn't going to get hit by the same punch a fifth time—so I sensed it and stepped away from Nakamura. If that reaction was any indication, I'd probably hit the nail on the head. He should just be honest about it.

"Tsk..."

"All right! We're here!"

Izumi gazed at the attraction ahead. Seen from below as it ran around in every direction at incredible speed, it had punch. Just as the name implies, you could hear the screams of the riders from here.

And then we caught sight of some people who'd just gotten off the ride. They tottered on by, going, "Whoa..." They were clearly exhausted, and some of them were even sweating.

Izumi blinked as she watched them. "...So what do we do? ...Are we really riding this?"

"Hey, you're the one who suggested it," Nakamura shot back at her.

Now that even I was ribbing on him, he was being snippy with her, too.

* * *

It was about half an hour after we'd gotten in line for the most popular ride, Hollywood Fire Fright. Finally, after just a few more groups, it would be our turn.

"This kinda has an atmosphere, huh?"

"Ah, everyone's all scared."

The interior of the ride was a reproduction of the aesthetic of a Hollywood movie, and as the line moved along, it gradually got darker and more eerie. The human-skeleton decorations placed along the cave-like hallway seemed to hint at the frights to come, and we were getting jittery.

"W-we're almost there...," Kikuchi-san said beside me.

"Yeah. You all right?"

"I'm scared...but the excitement is stronger." Though she was scared, she was facing forward with interest. She really does have the character of a writer—she's the type who's more curious than anything else at times like these.

Since we'd come here straight after opening, it had been a short wait to get right up to almost boarding despite this being the most popular ride—just as Izumi expected. Apparently, if we'd come a little later, we would have been waiting an hour to a hundred minutes, so maybe it really had been the right idea to go early. Just what you'd expect from a serious theme-park aficionado.

But seeing people coming off the ride had gotten Izumi freaked out now. "O-oh no...my heart's beating faster..."

Concerned for her, Kikuchi-san tried to encourage her. "Are you all right...?" The archangel Kikuchi-san is overflowing with kindness.

And then—my eye caught Hinami, who was a little behind them, zoning out looking ahead on the line.

I took a few steps forward. "...Hinami."

"Hmm?"

She looked a little surprised that I was suddenly talking to her. This was the first time on this trip that I'd approached her to chat.

I didn't think she was going to open up to me right this minute. But I still wanted to talk with her a bunch of times until I could get something out of her.

"You aren't scared of these things?"

"...Hmm, well...," she said, pausing to consider a bit. Was she taking time to think about the question I'd asked, or was she surprised that I was suddenly talking to her now? Well, she'd never replied to that message I'd sent her on LINE a week ago, so it was clear that she was avoiding me. She probably wasn't very willing to talk to me.

"Actually, when I went to theme parks before, I didn't really go on the roller coasters. So I don't really know!"

"...Oh."

What I got, of course, was just the meaningless remarks that came from her mask. I couldn't complain when I'd been the one to approach her, but the way Hinami interacted with me in this situation really hurt.

It made me feel like the more we talked, the further we got from anything real.

But the kid calling out "happy birthday" had surprised her, so if we kept conversing like this, maybe I would eventually find a way in.

Hoping for her mask to crumble, I said, "I'm hoping that you'll be so scared, you sob your eyes out."

"Ah-ha-ha. *You'd* better not run away before we get on."

I still hadn't managed to have a conversation with the real Hinami, but I just had to slowly make my voice reach further inside. Testing out what sort of debuffs work is just basic strategy for defeating a boss.

* * *

"W-we're finally here?!"

Takei's cry made me lift my head, and before I knew, we were next.

Then right as we were steeling ourselves for the ride—

—suddenly, the staff member guiding people onto the ride saw Hinami's stickers and called, "Ohh! Happy birthday!"

How many times had a stranger said that since we'd come to USJ? Ten times at least.

"Ah-ha-ha. Thank you," Hinami replied, clearly used to it by now.

Then in an even brighter tone, the staff member said, "Since it's your special day, please sit at the very back! That's the birthday seat!"

"Huh?"

"That's where it really feels like you're flying through the air! It's the scariest! It's empty right now, so please go ahead!"

I could see the expression on Hinami's mask freeze up then.

This coaster went backward, meaning the very back was actually the very front.

"Ahh...um..."

Her expression froze, and there was a slightly too-long pause, as if she was looking for an excuse.

Hmm, I think I know what's going on here. "That look says you don't want to do it," I said.

"...So what?"

"!" Seeing Hinami's expression, I was gleeful.

I mean, that cold remark, that sharp expression and tone of voice—that was a little different from the perfect heroine that she played in the class. It was close to the girl I'd met in Sewing Room #2—to NO NAME.

I prodded her again, same way as before. "Don't tell me...you're chicken?"

I wanted to talk with this Hinami a little more.

During summer vacation, Hinami had given me the assignment of teasing people, and I was good enough with this skill that I could use it with Nakamura. Now I was directing it at Hinami herself.

But I wasn't just going through formalities. This was to draw out how she really felt.

"You're more scared of this than I thought you'd be," I said.

Precisely speaking, this was directed at the other mask of hers called NO NAME, which had peeked out just a little from behind the thick mask of Hinami.

She sighed and raised her eyebrows so that only I could see. "If you're going to be like that, then fine. I'll sit there… But…"

"Yeah?"

And then with the sadistic smile that she'd shown frequently these past few months, she said:

"—Of course, you'll be sitting next to me, right?"

"…Huh?"

"All right, then you two are in the last row! Go ahead, go ahead!"

"…Uhh?"

"Then happy birthday! Have a nice ride!"

Hinami and the staff shoved me over, and then the safety harness was clicked into place, and before I knew it, I couldn't move.

With Hinami and me in the last seat, the coaster started running backward.

"Ahhhhhh?!"

"Yeeeeeeek!"

And so Hinami's birthday and NO NAME's sadism pulled me into experiencing the terror of the rear seat.

* * *

"Urk…the ground…is spinning…"

After getting off the Hollywood Fire Fright backdrop, I was a zombie. I'd completely lost my senses.

And at my side, Hinami was tottering and swaying and completely green. There was none of the cool of the perfect heroine on her face now.

"Urk…that was worse than I expected…," she groaned.

"Yeah…"

Frankly, I'd underestimated it—a rear-facing roller coaster was scary in a way I kind of didn't expect. It keeps jolting you up and down, and you don't know which way you're going next, so you get yanked every which way without being able to brace for it.

And since we'd been in the back row, our view had been spinning around, and now my inner ear was all out of whack.

"This is because...you opened your big fat mouth...," grumbled Hinami.

"No, we wound up in the back row because of those birthday stickers."

"...Stop quibbling."

"Is that quibbling...?"

Though Hinami looked weak as we chatted, I felt a subdued joy.

The tone of her conversation, the way she addressed me—

—it was a little different from the way she spoke to me as the perfect heroine in class.

"Hmm, that was pretty fun..."

"Yeah, it was... Not bad at all."

A little ways away, Nakamura and Mizusawa were competing to see who could play it cooler, but they were both a little unsteady on their feet. You know, when you've got your pride as a man, you really can't complain. At the very least, it seemed they weren't paying attention to how Hinami's tone had turned a little cold with me. By the way, Takei was next to them loudly going on about how "that was so scary, right, guys?!" The guy's nothing if not honest and energetic.

"Uurk...maybe I can't handle roller coasters...," Mimimi groaned, despite usually being so chipper.

"That was wild, huh...," Izumi agreed, though she was the one who'd suggested we ride this in the first place. "No wonder it's the most popular..."

They were both completely wiped out. By my count, the majority of the group had been annihilated.

Meanwhile, Kikuchi-san and Tama-chan were the only ones full of energy.

"It was pretty fun, wasn't it?" Kikuchi-san said.

"Yeah!"

Hey, this isn't like what I imagined—can't we do something about this? Kikuchi-san should be the one feeling weak, and then I sweep in to support her. Kikuchi-san's strong...

Though Izumi was wobbling, she screwed up her strength. "O-okay, time for the next one!" She must have felt she had a mission to lead the ultimate USJ tour. Still a bit pale, she fervently reviewed some notes in her phone. She had the enthusiasm of an *Atafami* player pulling an all-nighter on training mode.

"So...what do we ride next?" Hinami asked with a rather imploring look toward Izumi. I could see in her eyes exactly what she was thinking: *Please no more scream machines; let's ride something more chill.*

"So next...," Izumi said while looking at her phone.

"Umm, my notes say...it's time for Air Force Dinosaur!"

"That's a bad one, too, right?!" Hinami cried out loud, unusually for her. You never got to see that expression on her when she was the perfect heroine Hinami or NO NAME Hinami.

I wasn't the only one to notice that—Izumi, Mizusawa, and everyone else stared at Hinami.

Eventually, Izumi burst into laughter. "—Ah-ha-ha!"

"Wh-what...?"

And then after cackling for a while, Izumi wiped her eyes as if she was relieved. "...I'm just glad you're having fun, Aoi."

"Just what about this makes you think I'm having fun?!" Hinami was once again thrown into dismay.

Izumi was getting carried away now. "All right, it's settled! Next is Air Force Dinosaur! Everyone, follow me!"

"Why?! Hey, Yuzu?!"

Watching as the meaning of the Make Hinami Happy Championship changed under Izumi's leadership, I silently cheered her on. *Nice, do that some more. But please avoid dragging me into it too much.*

* * *

It was about half an hour later.

After two scream machines back-to-back, we were firmly divided into three camps.

"Wow, that was amazing, huh?"

"Yeah. You handled that pretty well, too, Takei."

"The view was so beautiful!"

We were sitting divided into groups at the open terrace of a café in the Hollywood area, where we all ordered drinks. Of these groups, Takei, Tama-chan, and Kikuchi-san were sitting at the table of the powerful. All three of them had cleared the trial with no damage. They were such a mismatched trio, it felt like a glitch in the system.

"Urk...Tama...run..."

Mimimi, Izumi, Nakamura, and I were at the table beside them. My inner ears were totally screwed up; I was just trying to recover by getting some air. Mimimi looked particularly beat—even though Tama-chan was about to fall to Takei's clutches, she was helpless to do anything.

"You guys are all pathetic! Maybe just us three will go another round!"

"Ah-ha-ha, maybe we could."

"No...Tama...watch out..."

Tama-chan was on the verge of being taken away by Takei, and Mimimi could do nothing. I really wanted to laugh, but my head was spinning too much.

—These seven were sitting at these two tables, which meant...

"That's a flaw of yours, huh, Takahiro?"

"Ha-ha-ha, well, I have no plans to fix it."

...sitting at the other table were Mizusawa and Hinami.

The two of them had seemed about as hard-hit as us right after getting

off the coaster, but they'd gradually recovered. By the way, Izumi had originally been at that table, too, but she'd just moved over to us.

"Izumi...why are you over here...?" I asked her.

"Huh? Uhhh, well..."

Izumi had recovered better than me and Mimimi. She lowered her voice a bit to say, "Hey...I think Takahiro wants to make a play for Aoi on this trip."

"?!"

Her guess cut so close to the truth, I just about bit my tongue. How can she have such a sharp intuition for romance? I guess people get good at what they like?

"So...I thought I'd give them some time alone together!"

"O-oh..."

Though I kind of had complicated emotions about it, I did want to support Mizusawa's efforts to reach her. But if that took up Hinami's time, then I'd lose my chance for us to talk about our feelings again.

But even without that, I still had strangely complicated feelings. I wanted to welcome the two of them getting together, so I didn't know why.

"...Yeah. I hope it goes well," I said. Part of that was definitely sincere, but there was probably a part that wasn't.

"Right?!"

By the way—oh yeah, Nakamura wasn't participating in the conversation at all—

"...Urk."

—and that was 'cause he was facedown on the table. He'd been hit harder than all of us.

* * *

By now, everyone had recovered, Nakamura included.

We were sitting on the same open terrace, and we were finally feeling good enough for lunch as well as drinks.

Izumi said that just about all the restaurants would be packed by seven, so we could explore more efficiently if we had an early lunch and went around to the attractions while everyone else was having lunch. And right now was just past eleven—perfect scheduling. The way she'd mastered this route—she was a training-mode demon.

We opened the menu to find it was mainly light foods such as sandwiches and cake—perfect for recovering from the damage we'd just been hit with. Izumi had been the one to choose this place, but if she'd even anticipated the fare in her selection, then she's really at the top of the Elite ranking.

We picked what we liked from the menu and ordered. Then—

"Happy birthdaaaay!"

Izumi must have arranged for it—another server lady brought a piece of cake with a lit sparkler stuck in it.

Naturally, Hinami was getting used to repeated birthday congratulations, and she responded, "Thank you!" without getting flustered. The same tactic won't work over and over again on a first-class gamer—or so I was thinking, when...

"It's this young lady right here's birthday!" The server lady addressed everyone on the open terrace, including the other guests.

"Huh?"

"Let's all sing for her! One, two! Happy birthday to you... ♪"

And so the server led the song, and the other customers around us were drawn into it. The special feeling of being in a theme park must have helped, as everyone was pretty willing to sing the birthday song for Hinami. She must not have imagined it would go this far, as she seemed a little surprised, but she quickly got into it and started singing with a broad smile on her face.

And then our group all stood up and faced Hinami, clapping our hands as we sang. Since it was an open terrace, passersby who were into it started joining in, too. *Ha-ha, what the heck is this?*

And then a crowd of a few dozen people had formed around this corner, and their smiles, goodwill, and celebratory song were all directed at Aoi Hinami alone.

"Ah-ha-ha…"

There were some high school girls around our age who were doing USJ-niforms, some outgoing guys in red, blue, and green hoodies and headbands, some girls dressed as wizards waving around wands like conductors' batons, and then even some really realistic dinosaurs gathered around, too. It was probably staff inside them, coming over to celebrate Hinami's birthday.

Of course, Hinami had never had "Happy Birthday" sung to her by a large crowd of strangers and dinosaurs. She accepted the singing with a shy smile on her face, clapping quietly herself as well. Actually, what *is* the right thing to do at a time like this?

"Ha-ha-ha. This is impressive." Mizusawa laughed pleasantly.

Frankly, I'm sure opinions are divided on this kind of thing. If I got this as a surprise, I think I'd be glad but also feel uncomfortable. But apparently, getting slammed with celebration like this was just right for Hinami.

Well, you'd have to do this, or the wave of celebration wouldn't reach the real Hinami under her thick mask. Izumi is really gutsy for trying to overload her this way.

"…Happy birthday tooo yoouuuu!"

The song came to a close with the audience about three times as large as it was at the start.

And Hinami was ready for it—at just the right moment, she blew out the sparkler on the cake. "Fwoooo!"

"Happy birthday, Aoi!"

"Happy birthday, miss!"

"Graaaaaoowr…!"

"This sure is happy!"

"Happy b-day, Aoi."

And so with birthday congratulations being showered on her from us, from the dinosaurs, and from strangers, Aoi said, "I get it, thank you! This is so embarrassing!" Her brow was furrowed, but her expression was slowly edging toward a smile.

* * *

After that exciting meal, we headed to our next goal.

"That was pretty wild, huh, Aoi?" Tama-chan commented to Hinami.

"Too wild! Agh!" It seemed that the effects of the singing earlier were still lingering with her. If my estimation was correct, then it was also getting deeper into Hinami's sturdy mask and her armor.

I was wanting to believe in the possibilities of this trip.

The next place that we arrived was—

"Wooow! I didn't know they had something like this!" Hinami was surprised.

Izumi huffed smugly. "Yup! Actually, not many people know about this…"

Before us was a little shop, and being sold there was…

"Then one cheese-curry-flavored turkey leg!" Hinami said with cheer. That sounded frighteningly heavy.

Hey, just barely ten minutes ago, she was totally drained. And didn't we just eat, too?

"Hinami…you're still eating?" I said, trembling in fear.

But Hinami seemed fine as she accepted the giant hunk of meat. It was some really powerful-looking meat: a big smoked drumstick thickly drizzled in curry and yellow cheese, with red sauce on top.

"What're you talking about? Sweets and cheese are *hexactly* what I want right now."

"You mean like you have a second stomach for it?"

When you talk about having a second stomach, that's supposed to be for desserts, not cheese. In fact, cheese is one of those foods that's hard to fit in if you're not hungry.

"No quibbling. You can only eat these here, so I've got to have one."

She was saying it almost like it was an obligation. She's got way too much cheese on the brain.

"O-oh, really…?"

"Here we g—" Hinami was right about to eat it.

"The rich aroma of spices… I can't resist it…!" Mimimi zoomed in like a giant flying squirrel.

She was just clobbered by the roller coasters, so why…? I wondered—but oh yeah, she'd been suffering so much before, she'd hardly had anything to eat for lunch. Now that she'd recovered, she was understandably tempted by the smell of curry.

"Ahh!"

Mimimi swooped in to bite into Hinami's turkey leg, and then Hinami bit into the other side—two track stars sharing a single turkey leg.

"Ohh! Nice! Both of you, stay like that!"

"Huh? Hike at?!" Hinami's remark was muffled by her mouth full of turkey.

Izumi brought up her phone camera and started snapping some Instagrammable photos of them.

Mimimi was saying, "Hwill?!" which I think was her saying, *Still?!*

"Then next…let's try one up through your lashes!" Izumi was totally into being the cameraman, and after taking shots in a few different variations, she said, "Okay, I got some nice ones… Wait, huh?"

Swiping through the photos, Izumi noticed it first, and eventually, Hinami and Mimimi also picked up on it.

"Huh?"

"Hmm?"

All three gazes focused on the ground right under them. There, a yellow and red mass was crushed flat.

Either it had been the girls holding a slightly forced pose for a while, or maybe it had fallen off while they were taking the variety of shots. Unwittingly, the cheese topping had fallen on the ground.

"S-sorry…," said Mimimi.

"No, I was the one who told you to hold the pose…," Izumi replied, also trying to take responsibility.

But Hinami's head was hanging as she handed over the plain, boring turkey leg over to Mimimi. "No…it's okay. Mimimi, if you're hungry, you can have this…" Hinami was morose now. If there was no more cheese, then she didn't need it anymore.

"Umm…," said Mimimi, like she wasn't sure what to say.

"Don't worry about it… I'm fine…" With an expression that was clearly not fine, Hinami started trudging back the way we'd come.

And then—

"'Scuse me, another of the same."

"You're buying it again?!"

Hinami's obsession with cheese knew no bounds.

* * *

And then we finally arrived.

"Ah! Over there!" Tama-chan found the distant entrance, and everyone focused to just barely see it. Tama-chan's got good eyes.

We walked about another minute from there, and then Takei started freaking out. "Whooooooooooa! It's a big pipe!"

He was certainly right about that. The entrance before us was made like the green pipe that Yontendo's figurehead character used to move around. We were all very excited.

"Ohhh! It's so well-made!" Mimimi cried out.

"It's like we're in the game!" Tama-chan said, and the rest of us agreed.

We'd gotten boarding tickets using the phone app while we were lined up for the first attraction, so we showed those to the staff and went inside.

Once we'd gone a ways inside, I was really impressed. "Whoaaaa!"

Inside the pipe, lights like those of a warp hole started running by us.

"Wow! It's so pretty! Is this how the pipes work?" Hinami said, gazing at the lights.

"I was thinking the same thing," I said.

"Yeah? Ha-ha."

The pipes did warp him to other places—so that meant there were actual warp holes inside? That had never occurred to me.

We passed through the light to enter a room that looked like something in a castle… Wait.

"It's the *64* castle!" I cried out.

"It is!" Hinami replied.

Clearly, we were the only two getting excited about this. *Is this okay?*

It was a faithful re-creation of the entrance to the castle, which was the player's base in the game that could be called Yontendo's masterpiece.

"Whoa… This is almost too much," I said.

"I get that…but then what's coming next will be too much for you to handle."

Hinami and I were talking about video games with the innocence of children. The way she was opening up now, it was like that rocky period between us had never happened. You wouldn't imagine she'd ignored my LINE messages for a week. Suddenly, we were walking at the head of the group. And in our typically individualistic way, we were going off on our own to check out the things we wanted to see.

And then at the end of it, when we came out to the other side—

"—!"

Spread before us was a sight that didn't seem like real life.

It was a toylike world, like the screen of a game brought straight into reality. From the brick bridges and apple trees to even the grass on the ground, this world was made with a texture like plastic model figures. This was reality, but it sure didn't feel like it.

There were coins that spun around, chestnut-shaped enemies that went back and forth in place, flowers with teeth that grew from the pipes. The world that I'd adored since I was a child had been reproduced with love, and everything in it moved in a familiar-looking way. The boss castle looming in the background had a tall entrance in the shape of a turtle's face—you might think the design would seem childish, but right now it was incredible, even beautiful.

"Whoa! That's so cool!"

"Wooow!"

Hinami and I cried out at the same time.

That must have snapped Hinami out of her spell. We looked at each other, and then she jerked her face away grumpily.

I couldn't help but laugh. "...Ha-ha."

Of course, I was glad that she was just as pleased by this as I was. But more than that, the way she'd jerked her face away—it meant that she'd had a moment of sincere joy that she felt she had to hide.

Kikuchi-san arrived just a moment later. "...This is really wonderful," she said kindly. That made me take another good look at the sights.

Hinami and I had always said that the world is like a video game.

That was largely metaphorical. But now, in the real sense, this world had become a video game.

Everyone was coming in one after another. "This is exciting, huh?!" Takei was getting loud and emotional.

"Huh, this is pretty well-made." Mizusawa looked around like he was impressed.

In this case, it seemed like Mizusawa was impressed at how thoroughly the attractions were put together. He wasn't really the gaming type, as far as I could tell.

And then there was Nakamura.

"...!"

He probably had considerable affection for video games. His mouth was hanging half-open as he took in this world, blinking his eyes. He wasn't saying anything, but his expression spoke more eloquently than anything else. *I get that, I understand your feelings.*

"Look! That flower enemy! It's bigger than you, isn't it, Tama?!" Mimimi crowed.

"You don't have to compare us," Tama-chan shot back.

As everyone was expressing wonder in their own ways, Kikuchi-san alone was silent, watching everyone.

Well, maybe not everyone, but—

I came up by her side. She continued to look somewhere else but stepped closer to me. "Hinami-san was really glad, wasn't she?" she said, neither about me nor herself.

"...Yeah. You think so, too?"

"Yes. It didn't seem like acting or anything like that."

"...I see." Her agreement gave me courage. "Then it's a good thing we chose this place."

"...Yes, it is."

And then with a slightly complicated expression, Kikuchi-san said, "I'm...glad, too." She seemed like she was kind of forcing herself to speak in a certain way. Then she smiled gently.

* * *

"Wow! There's some more here, too!"

I don't know if it was because she figured she'd already shown us her childlike side once or she'd decided to defiantly embrace it, but Hinami was enjoying Yontendo World more than ever.

"Ah-ha-ha, so many coins are coming out!"

At Yontendo World, there's these bands you can buy at the shop that can be synced with a phone app, enabling you to access a bunch of gimmicks—like when you hit the blocks that were placed in certain areas, you could get coins in the app. Right now, Hinami was whacking one of those blocks over and over with a grin on her face.

"You're right! ...Wow, this is surprisingly soft."

"Well, I'm sure that's so the kids don't hurt themselves."

"Huh, I'm not sure if you're destroying the magic here or not."

Hinami had gone into innocent-child mode, and I was the only one who could keep up with her enthusiasm.

"Aoi…kinda seems like she's having fun," Tama-chan said.

"Yeah…more than when she's at track," Mimimi agreed.

I could hear what they were saying, but having fun wasn't a bad thing, so I pretended like I didn't notice.

Hinami and I took the lead in enjoying the attractions of Yontendo World. We played a game where you all work together to stop an alarm clock from waking up a tough flower enemy, and we went through a maze to find pieces of a puzzle that you complete at the final door.

We enjoyed the place to the fullest, as if the earlier exhaustion from the roller coaster had never happened.

"Complete! Now we get the key."

"All right!"

Then Hinami and I got all the keys that you can get by clearing the various attractions and completed all the miniattractions. *Heh-heh-heh, this is what happens when my gamer blood gets going.*

As I was just having myself a good time, I noticed Izumi and Mizusawa watching me from a little ways away. I looked over to see the two of them grinning and sticking up their thumbs as if to say, *Nice!*

This trip had started with the goal of surprising Aoi Hinami and making her happy.

In that sense, Hinami appeared to be enjoying this place now more than any other time we'd seen. *Heh, so then I was the one to make her happy, after all.*

* * *

And then after enjoying ourselves a while, we decided to take a break.

While everyone was going to look at merch or going to the washroom, I stopped by a café in Yontendo World. It was getting to evening. We'd had an early lunch, so I was getting a little hungry. But since it wasn't quite mealtime, I decided to get a hot parfait drink with pudding to go, then eat it outside the café.

Once I was done ordering, I was gazing at the USJ app in satisfaction with the parfait drink in hand when Kikuchi-san walked up by my side.

"How is it going?" she said.

"Hey, Kikuchi-san."

And then I proudly showed her my phone screen. "Look. I got all the keys."

"Tee-hee. You really looked like you were having fun."

"Yep."

"Both you and Hinami-san."

"…Yeah." I nodded.

Kikuchi-san put a hand to her chest, and in her usual gentle tone, as if she was telling a story, she said, "Maybe…it would have been good to do this for Alucia, too."

"Umm, what do you mean?" I asked.

While glancing over toward Hinami, Kikuchi-san said, "A sort of heroic boy feeling very thankful for what she's given him and taking her around someplace fun. Just dragging her into it, even if she protests." With appreciation for the world, Kikuchi-san went on. "His friends are all there, too, and everyone's completely doting on her." The way she was talking, she seemed to be holding something close to her heart, even if it meant letting go of something else. "Then maybe Alucia wouldn't have had to worry about not having blood."

"…Yeah, maybe."

That kinda made sense to me, but it still felt a little off. I didn't know how much of what Kikuchi-san was saying fit the story of reality.

"Thank you, Fumiya-kun." Kikuchi-san smiled.

I nodded without a word, then gently teased her. "But that's not quite what's going on here, Kikuchi-san."

"Hmm?"

Our surprise had only just begun.

"We're only just getting to the plan."

"Tee-hee." Kikuchi-san laughed. "That's true... Let's make sure she has a great time."

"Of course." I nodded with confidence, and I started thinking about our scheme.

That was when something caught my eye.

"...Found?!"

I yelped without thinking.

From the café window, I could see the center of Yontendo World, a square used as a relay point for various attractions.

And there had suddenly appeared a life-size ninja character striking poses—Found, who Hinami and I had both used when we had met over *Atafami*.

"H-hey! Hinami! Hinami!" I called out for her and raced out for the person who would most share my excitement.

Hinami was alone a little ways away by a vending machine, buying a drink. "Huh? What is it?"

"It's Found! Found!" I was so worked up, I wasn't being very clear, but I was able to communicate the most important term.

"Found... Wait, you mean..."

That was when she got it, and she looked over to the center of Yontendo World. "...!"

It was a voiceless expression of joy. Hinami's eyes sparkled like any girl meeting her favorite celebrity.

I considered teasing her for a moment, but I immediately dropped the idea. I mean, you shouldn't deny someone's love for a video game character, and besides—this was NO NAME, the top player who loved *Atafami* with all her heart.

"Guys! They're doing a meet 'n' greet!" Izumi called out as she ran toward us.

"A what?" I called back.

"A meet and greet!" she shouted again from a distance. Her eyes were sparkling.

I tried to remember the USJ info that I'd researched beforehand. "Wait, we can talk to them?!"

"Yeah!"

While talking with Izumi, who was a few meters away, I looked to the side. There was Hinami, eyes sparkling like an eager child. Her gaze was fixed on Found, who was energetically darting from pose to pose to put on a show for the fans.

Someone's easy to understand. "Hinami."

"What?"

"Let's go meet Found!"

Maybe I sounded too gleeful, as Hinami gave me a sullen look. "...That's just someone in a character suit," she said, a flatly realist remark that the perfect heroine would never say.

"Ha-ha...just like you. Except your suit is slipping," I snarked back at her.

"Sh-shut up," Hinami scowled.

But that was fine with me. I wanted to talk lots with Hinami when she was out of character.

I lightly took her by the arm and started walking.

"Hey?!"

I pulled her along, one step after another, till we were close to Found. "Look, this is our character, right?" I said.

She gave me a sullen glare. "...anged yours."

"Huh?"

"...You changed yours to Jack," she complained petulantly. After that brief remark, she pouted and sulked.

Frankly, I was thinking, *That's what you're mad about?* But I was glad that I could talk about *Atafami* with Hinami again.

"Ha-ha...sorry about that."

An honest apology seemed to satisfy her, and she resisted my pull a little less.

Well, I'm sure it was the right choice to apologize for that. To us *Atafami* players, changing your main is a big deal.

"Fine," she said. "...I get it, so let go of my arm."

"Okay. Sorry."

Then we met up with Izumi. "Everyone's coming now!" she said, then zoomed off somewhere.

I was a little unsure what to do, but seeing that Hinami's eyes were focused only on Found, I figured there was one answer. "Can't wait, can you?" I said smugly.

"Well...you said it." Hinami seemed disgruntled, but when I walked out, she followed after me.

"Sure, sure, roger."

Yeah, this closeness, this warmth—

—this was comfortable for me.

So just Hinami and I went up to Found. And then...

...Apparently noticing Hinami's birthday sticker, Found reached out with exaggerated surprise and rushed up to Hinami. And then after a wordless approach like something out of a flashy musical number, the ninja dropped to one knee and welcomed Hinami with open arms in celebration.

After the enthusiastic display, Hinami giggled like a child. "...Hey, don't you think a ninja should draw less attention?"

Standing there was not at all perfection, but just a sharp-tongued gamer who loved *Atafami*.

"Hey, they're doing it for you, so don't complain."

I quipped back and forth with this Hinami with pleasure.

* * *

Not long after that, Izumi raced around the area to gather the group here, and once she had everyone, she made a proposal. "Hey, since we're all here, we should take a group photo!"

Of course, I was down with Izumi's suggestion, so I jumped on her idea. "Yeah! We can do that, right?" I confirmed enthusiastically with everyone.

Everyone nodded, and we asked Found, "Can we take a picture?" And then the staff lady who was nearby told us with cheer, "Thank you very much! That will be fifteen hundred yen!"

Hinami said so only I could hear, "So they charge, huh?"

What a thing to say. Her hidden side is so nasty.

"That's inevitable. Our Found is just that popular."

"Not yours anymore."

"You're still saying that…"

Even our whispered jabs back and forth—I wanted those, too.

We handed our phones to the staff lady, and we lined up around Found, with Hinami in the middle.

"Then I'm taking the photo! Okay, cheese!"

And that was when Found pulled a little party cracker out of his pocket and—

—*Bang!*

Colorful confetti blasted out at Hinami.

The shutter snapped at that exact moment, and that moment was captured in the shot.

"Ah-ha-ha! That startled me!" Hinami said like she was amused, and everyone laughed.

When the staff handed back the phone, it showed Hinami in the moment her broad smile turned to surprise; Mizusawa, who had instantly sensed something was up and had taken a step back; Nakamura and

Takei, who hadn't noticed anything; Mimimi and Izumi, who had both hands up to frame Hinami; and Tama-chan and Kikuchi-san, who were smiling from a step away.

And then there was me standing there like a stick, the moment I blinked perfectly captured.

"Ah-ha-ha! That's some really bad timing there, Brain!"

"Sh-shut up…"

Hinami was teasing me, too. "But it's very you."

"Come on, what makes you think this usually happens?"

Even with everyone making jabs at me, I realized that the sense of dissonance in my conversations with Hinami was now gone.

"Hey, Hinami." There was something I wanted to do with her. "Since I closed my eyes in that one, want to take another one?"

"Sure, I guess…"

"'Scuse me, could we do another one?"

Hinami nodded, but she was giving me a look that said she didn't know what I was planning.

Everyone else was watching to see what I'd do, too.

I grinned.

And then I made a pose at Found, like wrapping my whole arm with my fist around my neck, and then I slowly thrust that out.

"!"

Found's actor, a professional entertainer, also brought their fist up in a similar stance. I'm sure Hinami got it, but nobody else did.

"C'mon, Hinami," I said.

Though Hinami seemed momentarily hesitant, she was an *Atafami* fan and gave in to the temptation of doing this with Found. She was giving me that *Oh, if you insist* look on her face, but she came up to me and Found, and then—

—the back of my fist, Found's, and Hinami's all met in the air.

*　　*　　*

Once that moment had been saved in a photo, we thanked Found and left. When I checked the data in the phone I got back, there we were.

The photo had beautifully captured the three of us with the backs of our fists meeting as if in an attack.

And maybe it's weird to say of myself, but Hinami and I were both smiling like we were really enjoying that moment.

"Just how much do you love *Atafami*?" I teased.

"I don't want to hear that from you."

Sniping at each other like this was what I really wanted today.

*　*　*

We went through all the attractions at Yontendo World, and now all that was left was to get on the dinosaur-shaped ride that slowly toured around the whole area, Goshi's Adventure.

"Ah! It's our turn! Time to gooo!"

And so first went Izumi and Nakamura in the vehicles that slowly flew out over Yontendo World.

This ride was a two-seater, and it would have been fine to just pick whoever to ride with like we had been so far, but Izumi suggested that since this was the last ride, we should ride as couples. So first went Takei alone, and next Tama-chan and Mimimi departed together, and now Izumi and Nakamura were setting off. By the way, you could argue about whether you can call Tama-chan and Mimimi a couple, but I think they fit as a sort of two-in-one. I don't think there's any controversy about Takei being alone.

It was just me, Kikuchi-san, Hinami, and Mizusawa left.

"Yontendo World was really fun," I said as we lined up for the attraction, looking back on the day.

"It was. My inner gamer had a great time," said Hinami.

"Didn't know your inner gamer was so strong," Mizusawa cut in.

"Ah-ha-ha. Well, girls have many secrets."

Hinami and Mizusawa were having a rather nice little chat. Well, they're both very used to conversation, so they always have that air to them, but having heard Mizusawa's declaration before the trip, I felt like they'd gotten just a little closer.

The video game atmosphere was reproduced everywhere you looked, with dragons' eggs, big, cartoonish trees, and giant and colorful pancake things—everywhere were things that couldn't exist in real life. The arrow signs that showed where to go were the kind from the games, and my inner gamer was excited.

"Ohh, it's here. Then let's get on."

The next car had come, so I took the lead and stepped forward.

But right then...

"Yes. Then please get in."

"...Huh?"

...for some reason, Kikuchi-san, who would obviously be a set with me, had taken a step back.

And then—

"All right, Aoi, have a nice trip!"

"Huh?"

—with Mizusawa pushing her forward, Hinami was next up front. Then the staff prompted us, "Next two, please!" and Hinami was swept into the seat beside me.

"Hey, Kikuchi-san?! Mizusawa?!"

In the ride car, I turned back to see the two of them with very conspiratorial smiles.

"You owe me one, Fumiya. A big one," Mizusawa said with a triumphant grin.

"I'm a little jealous, but I want you to do this." Kikuchi-san also had a kind smile on her face.

"...Ah. I guess they set us up." Hinami sighed.

"You guys..."

Should he be prioritizing me at a time like this, when he said he'd be confessing his feelings to her on this trip? And Kikuchi-san was always so worried about Hinami, but she did that for me...

Basically, they were trying to do something about our relationship, even if it meant making sacrifices themselves.

"...I see," I said to myself. It did make sense.

"What?" Hinami gave me a skeptical look.

I had to thank the two of them from the bottom of my heart.

"No, it's nothing... Well, since now we're here, let's enjoy ourselves."

And so what I'd been after this whole trip—time to have a talk alone with Hinami—finally arrived.

* * *

Hinami and I were riding on a dinosaur-shaped vehicle that slowly circled the outer perimeter of Yontendo World, where we'd had so much fun.

When we'd first got here, the refreshingly clear blue sky and the CG-like world had left an impression, but now it seemed kind of lonely in the sunset light.

"So...today," I began quietly.

The pale-blue streetlights shone at fixed intervals, gradually illuminating the unreality of this world—with blooming flowers as thick as seat pillows and apples that were glowing orange for some reason. The white glow from the question marks on the item blocks lit up the dazzling red, blue, and yellow primary colors of the other blocks and faintly mingled with the sunset.

It really was the world of the childish video game that we loved—but it was also reality.

"I'm glad you had fun," I said.

Hinami was still pouting, but she didn't seem bored at all, her eyes fixed on the clock telling us it was five PM. "That roller coaster was the worst, but this area...isn't bad."

"Ha-ha. Right?"

With the scowling enemy characters that fell down from above when you approached...

...the red turtles with innocent expressions, hovering with the wings that grew out of their shells...

...and this place, where the characters we'd seen thousands of times through the screen, were here to welcome us.

This place itself was a common language between Hinami and me.

"I was the one who said we should come here," I said. "I knew you'd love Yontendo World."

"...I see."

The conversation between us was stilted. The silence stood out, but maybe because of the world we loved surrounding us, it wasn't at all uncomfortable.

That was why I was able to guide the conversation into the core of our situation. "Hey...do you want to end your relationship with me?"

"I'm not really ending anything. I just did the obvious," Hinami said brusquely, but with none of her usual stubbornness.

"Obvious?"

"I don't regret it...but when you use someone else's life for yourself... that kind of relationship can't go on forever, right?" Hinami sounded resigned as she gazed at an enemy character hovering while blowing bubble gum. She seemed nostalgic, but also sad.

The look in her eyes felt a little different from when she was in Sewing Room #2 or when she was in the classroom.

"Because now you know...who I am."

There was a kind of self-rejection in her tone.

I didn't want to hear that from Hinami. That's why I drew in a breath and said, "Lately, I've been thinking." After hearing the opinions of adults like Ashigaru-san and Rena-chan, I'd come to understand something. "Basically, everyone, I think, has something like their own karma that other people won't understand."

The ride slowly approached a darkened indoor area, and our view became dimmer and more closed in.

"I get that. Because I'm the same as you," I said.

"...You mean that you try to deal with your own life yourself?" Hinami asked.

I nodded. "I'm an individualist. The more I try to make a relationship with someone special, the more it just goes wrong. And I hurt whoever was trying to get close to me. It means I leave the people I care about behind to go way off somewhere else. I think a lot of people don't understand."

Something I couldn't change about myself made it harder to connect. Or maybe I just couldn't reach a compromise with the world.

It brought pain with it, like it was denying who I am.

"But, like. That isn't just you and me," I continued.

"...What do you mean?"

Thinking of the people I'd been deeply involved with, I said, "Kikuchi-san is a writer down to her core. Even though she knows there's a line with people that you can't cross, that their minds should be respected...she sometime starts to feel okay with crossing that line for writing. That's her karma. I think she hasn't come to a compromise with the world in that."

Each person's karma would look a bit different, though.

"And Mizusawa, too. He performs formalities instead of going for something he really wants. He's good at playing the game, but he can't get serious about what's right in front of him. He's trying to change himself, but I think he still doesn't have an answer that satisfies him. So he just has to try things out one by one."

But in the sense of being in contradiction with the world, I'm sure anyone is the same.

"Tama-chan is like me in that she believes in herself even when she can't fully explain why, and she can't understand people who aren't like that in the real sense. And that's isolated her in the past... I think she's managing well now, but it's not like everything's resolved."

I think resolving those things is one of the themes of life.

"So—it's not just you. Everyone acts like they're fine in front of others, but they're actually not. Maybe what you're dealing with is really extreme, and just touching it hurts. But…"

I borrowed the ideas I'd gotten from Kikuchi-san to affirm Hinami.

"…you're not a different creature from everyone else."

Maybe Hinami and I…
In a different sense, maybe we were firelings.

"So you don't have to be alone."

When I told her how I really felt, Hinami's expression didn't change. She just gazed at the world of video games and reality that was spread below us.

"If that were really true, then maybe I could have had it easy."

She spoke with the firm assumption that she was right and basically rejected my whole speech.

But I didn't want to give up.

"Still, if you can't validate yourself…then it can be just a little bit. It can just be as much as you'll allow."

If she couldn't validate herself, then we should help each other.

Even if that crossed the boundaries of individualism.

"Won't you let me take on some of what you're dealing with?"

If two individuals both had the desire to cross that boundary line— then that should be fine.

After I said that, Hinami surveyed the world as if captivated by its beauty.

Was she looking at the beauty of this world, or the beauty of the video games in her memory? Or was it the beauty of taking the world as a game?

I didn't know.

But it had to be here and now.

We couldn't talk about some things unless we were encompassed by this view.

"You know, I had two younger sisters." The words spilled out of Hinami like a droplet of water.

"!" My breath caught.

That was probably a different topic from what we'd been discussing before.

I focused on what she was saying so as to catch every word, every twitch in her facial expression.

"All three of us were close... We played games every day. We played versus in *Oinko* a lot... Of course, I was older, so I was better." There was something childish about the way Hinami spoke, and it sounded like she felt nostalgic for that kind of fun. "Every time I won, every time 'hexactly' came up on the screen, they teased me and said their big sister was the Demon Lord Aoi. The final boss. Every single day."

I imagined what that looked like.

That had to be before Aoi Hinami had become NO NAME. Or maybe she was talking about before she'd become the warped perfect heroine.

"My middle sister... Her name was Nagisa. She had a strong sense of justice, and she believed in herself... She was like you and Hanabi that way." Her storytelling slowly became calmer. "When Nagisa was in elementary school...there was bullying in her class."

"...Oh."

For some reason, Hinami's tone wasn't somber at all. Something about that felt unnatural and artificial to me.

As if she was afraid of being swallowed up by the facts otherwise.

"Nagisa had a strong sense of justice, so she couldn't pretend she didn't see it. Even if it meant she would be the next target, she cared more about sticking to her beliefs."

"That's..."

"Like Hanabi, right?"

I nodded. At the same time, I remembered.

When Tama-chan had become the target of bullying, Hinami had exacted disproportionate revenge on Erika Konno.

"But there wasn't a happy ending like with Hanabi."

She explained as if it was nothing. As if she had to talk about it this way to keep from breaking.

"She died. It was a traffic accident."

"...An accident?"

Her sister had died. Somewhere in my head, I'd imagined it, ever since I'd gone with Kikuchi-san to ask about her past from a former classmate.

But now she was telling me it was a traffic accident—how was that connected with bullying?

I still couldn't imagine it.

"Hey, nanashi."

She suddenly used the name she'd used when we first met.

"Do you know what hurt the most about it?"

I'd meant to be asking about her, and now she turned it back on me. I flinched. Her eyes seemed to be asking me if I was prepared, capturing me tight and not letting me go.

"I'm guessing...it wasn't just losing the little sister you loved?"

"Of course there was that. But...not just that." Hinami was slowly starting to sound like she was talking about someone else. "The driver who hit Nagisa really regretted it. They were crying the whole time and said they'd

spend the rest of their life trying to make up for it. So I think they were telling the truth." She didn't sound quite like the perfect heroine or like NO NAME. "They said that Nagisa… She just wandered out into the road. No crosswalk or light nearby. Just suddenly drifted out into traffic." The gravity in her voice held me there, as if I was listening to the Aoi Hinami from that time.

"What do you think that means?" Hinami asked me.

"Why are you asking me?" All I could do was ask her a question instead.

Hinami sadly smiled.

"—Because I don't know."

Her voice made me think of someone flinging themselves into a lake.

"Maybe she was just tired. Maybe she was dizzy. Maybe a car came at the exact wrong moment and it was all a big coincidence…"

I was being dragged into deep blackness, where there were no hand-holds or hope.

"Or maybe it was all too much for her, and she did it on purpose."

I thought that was what it looked like from her point of view.

"Was it an accident, or suicide?"

Hinami's world was not gray.

"—I'll never know."

Maybe light had never shone there to begin with.

"…I see."

Even if I understood the meaning of her words, what she was saying still didn't feel real.

"So I don't even know what kind of regrets I should have. Should I have told her to sleep lots so she wouldn't get dizzy? Should I have told her to keep her head down during the bullying and protect herself first? If she was lonely, should I have told her she wasn't wrong, it's okay, you've got your big sister here with you—"

After a long speech blaming herself, she drew in a breath and let her voice steady out.

And then she laughed, as if at herself.

"I know what happened, but not why or where it started. So I have nothing to go on to make sense of it."

That was counter to the aesthetic that Hinami had always committed to.

"It was like Nagisa's death was completely separate from my world."

I thought that somehow resembled the way Hinami lived as a player.

"Like her death had been pushed out to some world beyond a screen. Whatever that is, it's somewhere I have no connection to."

The world she saw had reality and games all mixed up; even the past and future felt vague. When she spoke of the past, dragging the words out of her—she couldn't fully make sense of what had happened. Even her chance to grieve was taken from her.

She gazed out over the world in resignation. "There's no point in even talking about this, either," she said. It was like she was crushing her own dried-out heart in her hand.

"...I see."

I hesitated to answer too readily, or even to give her my thoughts.

But...

"Thank you for telling me."

"...It's nothing."

Hinami fell silent, and the dinosaur we were riding on circled back to the beginning.

I didn't think she was lying. But I didn't think that was all of Aoi Hinami's story, either.

Reality and video games, the past and the future, masks and truth.
Aoi Hinami and NO NAME.

Those few minutes wavered over various boundary lines, and once it
was over, we got off the ride, tossed out carelessly by the world into our
everyday lives.

The sand under my feet when I got off felt particularly gritty.

"—Come on, Tomozaki-kun. Let's go!" Hinami said brightly, a little
mask appearing on her face once more.

*　*　*

Now seven of us—it was minus Mimimi and Tama-chan, who had left
early to arrange the surprise—were at the Yontendo World gift shop.

"I want this! And this! But I don't have the money for it!" Takei cried.

"Ha-ha-ha, well, licensed merch can cost quite a lot," Mizusawa replied.

I was watching Takei and Mizusawa fool around like usual from a little
ways away. My body and spirit hadn't fully come back yet from Hinami's
past, and I was caught up in a sort of floaty feeling.

"Talk with Hinami about how we really feel."

I'd managed to accomplish the goal that I had come up with before
going on this trip.

I was sure this was just a small part of what she was dealing with, but
I'd been able to share a part of her story.

So then—for Hinami and me going forward—

—what could I change, now that I knew?

As I was thinking, my gaze was drawn to a corner of the shop.

Hinami was over with the character minis, studying them carefully.
She looked like she could vanish at any moment. That was probably just
because I still had feelings I hadn't dealt with.

There were already a number of mugs in the shopping basket hanging
from Hinami's hand.

I watched as Izumi approached her then.

"Oh! That's the ninja from before!" Izumi addressed her brightly.

"You noticed? Sure is," Hinami replied calmly.

There was a large illustration of the character we loved, Found, on the mug that she held up to show Izumi.

"You getting gifts?" Izumi asked.

Hinami averted her eyes like it was hard for her to say. "...Yeah." Eventually, she nodded slowly.

"This one is for my sister."

Hinami's tone was lower than usual.

Izumi must have taken that as fatigue from the trip, as she didn't treat it as out of the ordinary. "...Ohh! Is that right?" she answered, and then she started rummaging around on a nearby shelf.

I took a few steps up to them, but I wasn't able to talk with Hinami again.

I'd noticed her shopping basket—

—and the three mugs inside it.

* * *

"Waahhhh! I wanna have more fun!"

"Then should we leave you behind?"

"Don't leave me alone!"

It was seven in the evening. There was still time until USJ closed, but we were leaving now for the party.

"I'm glad we were able to ride everything we wanted to! The big roller coasters were pretty scary! Just a little!" Izumi said jokingly.

Kikuchi-san nodded. "I enjoyed myself a lot... Thank you very much," she said politely.

Everyone responded casually with things like "It's fine!"

"Right. I had fun, too," said Hinami.

"You *really* seemed like you were having a good time, Aoi," Mizusawa shot at her.

"You have a problem with that, Takahiro?"

Were they able to have a lighthearted exchange like that because they'd gotten closer through this trip, or was it really just an extension of the skills and formalities they'd already mastered? I didn't know. I've grown a lot, but I know I'll never be able to see into the depths of people's hearts.

And so after having fun at USJ, we left.

It's always sad to leave an amusement park. I think it's childish to want the fun to go on forever, but that urge hadn't changed even now that we were in high school.

It's got to be a human instinct, the fear of the magic spell wearing off.

But today was different—what came next was actually the main event.

"That was so much fun! I want to come again someday!" Hinami said, putting on a bright tone of voice and expression.

I hope she really means that, I thought.

5

Even when you think you've won, the demon lord often has another form

"Mizusawa...thanks for before."

We had left USJ and checked in to the guest house. I was sharing a room with Mizusawa, a dormitory room that had bunk beds plus a little space. We were casually sitting on a bed, where I got straight to expressing my thanks.

"Were you able to have a talk?" he asked.

"...Yeah. Thanks to you." I nodded.

"Great." Mizusawa grinned.

"Have you confessed—?" I began, but then I reconsidered and stopped. "There was no time you could've done that, huh... Sorry."

Then Mizusawa laughed. "Ha-ha-ha. I didn't expect Aoi to get dragged into so much."

"That's true... Well, I can't talk."

Starting from the happy-birthday stickers and the roller coaster at the beginning to Yontendo World, I felt like Hinami had let us peek under her mask like she never had before, thanks to our goodwill and affection and just a little bit of mischief.

"I think Aoi honestly enjoyed herself more than I expected, so I'm glad," Mizusawa said.

Thinking back on Hinami's behavior that day, I nodded. "Well, I can get that." Then I grinned conspiratorially.

"I've been thinking," Mizusawa said, reflecting. "What Yuzu's doing is clearly common formalities, right? Picking the most popular ride, getting a surprise cake—that's totally conventional stuff." There was a crooked smile on his face, but nothing dark in his words. "…But since we really tried to have fun with it, we got her to smile."

I sensed nothing like envy.

It was like he'd found a glimpse of what he wanted, and now he was trying to pin down the shape of it. "Even if it started with formalities," he said slowly, "we genuinely got into it."

It made me remember a major favor from a little while ago. "Mizusawa."

"Yeah?"

"It's probably the same thing."

"…Same as what?"

His words had done the same thing for me before.

They'd been all formality and bluff, no substance, but they'd helped me.

"The speech you made to Ashigaru-san and Endo-san," I said with gratitude and respect.

Mizusawa smiled. "…Oh, really?" Enthusiasm lit up his expression— and I was probably the cause. "Yeah. It was like a game, trying to figure out the best way to BS… You'd think it was just the sort of meaningless stuff I'm good at…" He smiled innocently.

"But I was able to get your very first sponsor. Gotta say, I'm kinda happy about that."

"Mizusawa…"

And then he suddenly stood up, as if whatever had possessed him was gone. "Okay, I get it. I'll use what I'm good at a little more to forge a way somehow."

"…Yeah."

I didn't really get all of what he'd told me at the end, but I did get that it was constructive.

I should just support him in that. That's what I figured.

"Come on, is it about time to go?" said Mizusawa.

"Ah, oh yeah."

When we'd left USJ and arrived at this guest house, Mimimi and Tama-chan had said, *"We're still getting ready. Hold on for about an hour until the party starts."* Looking at the clock, just about an hour had passed.

Then there was a *knock, knock* on the door.

"Come in," Mizusawa replied.

The doorknob rattled, and Mimimi cheerily poked her head in. "We're ready! Come to the first floor with fluttering hearts!"

"Sure thing."

"Roger."

And so finally began the real main event for the day.

* * *

"Happy birthdaaaay, Aoi!" Mimimi cried out, signaling a *bang, bang, bang* of crackers.

Aoi Hinami's surprise party had finally begun.

We were gathered in the living room–like shared space on the first floor of the guest house.

The room had four big three-seater sofas facing each other and two low tables between them. The colors were all white or wood grain, including the rug below, making the area feel clean and warm.

Not only was there a projector on the wall, there was also a kitchen right beside it. Tama-chan was there, working at something.

"Man, this has really been a nice day," Mizusawa said in an easygoing manner as he sat on a white upholstered sofa.

"Come on. I'm used to hearing happy birthday today, you know? I heard it from kids, from the staff, and from dinosaurs, too."

"Hey now, but we say it with more heart than any of them!" cried Mimimi.

"Ah-ha-ha. Yeah, maybe that's true. Thanks," Hinami responded with a teasing smile that showed a hint of vulnerability.

Was it because we'd had that conversation at Yontendo World, or just my imagination? I felt like Hinami's attitude was softer and more open than usual. But in a sense, that forced me to remember the darkness behind it.

...No, this isn't the time to be thinking about that.

We just had to make Hinami happy with this surprise, have it resonate with her.

That was what I wanted to do.

"All right, guys, then everyone must be getting hungry by now!" Mimimi started officiating.

"We're real hungry," Nakamura heckled her.

"Then it's the birthday dinner you've all been waiting for! Tama, you do the honors!"

Mimimi's call signaled Tama-chan to bring in plates of various dishes. Tama-chan must not have been able to carry it all, as Takei was helping her set the tables. On the other hand, it would be a disaster if the two of them got closer through this trip, so we really have to protect her.

"Huh...is this...?" Seeing the food that had come out, Hinami was surprised.

"Ohh?! Has she noticed?!"

"...The cheese penne we ate in Omiya?"

"Exactly right!" Mimimi said with a roaring laugh.

Hinami was smiling awkwardly, but she seemed glad. "Ah-ha-ha... wow."

"It's a full-course meal re-creating all the delicious cheese dishes that we've had going out together!"

With that introduction from Mimimi, we understood.

Hinami picked up the dish of carbonara on the table. "So this carbonara is the one we had together after the track tournament last year?"

"That's right!"

"...That takes me back."

So it was from all the places that Hinami, Mimimi, and Tama-chan had gone before. Most likely, they had re-created and tried making those dishes that Hinami had liked, over the course of less than a month to prepare.

"Huh…?" My gaze was drawn to the salad that was sitting on the table. "Wait, is this salad from Kitayono?"

"Ohh! Amazing, a correct answer from Brain?! You got it! This is the Italian salad from Kitayono!"

"Ha-ha…for real?"

Even though it wasn't my birthday, I was enjoying this, too.

We had visited that restaurant at a turning point after Hinami had started coaching me on life strategy. It was a delicious Italian place that Hinami and I had both loved.

Call it memories or our history—there was just a lot in there.

…Wait, but more importantly…

I looked out over the various dishes that were lined up on the table.

Salad, carbonara, cheese penne, caprese salad.

All of them had to hold lots of memories for Hinami, Mimimi, and Tama-chan.

"Hey, Aoi, do you remember?" Tama-chan said, pointing to the cheese penne and caprese salad. "This is the first restaurant we went to when me, you, and Minmi just became friends."

"…Yeah, I remember."

"And remember? You suddenly ordered a cheese assortment, and cheese penne, and a caprese salad."

"Yeah," Hinami said.

With much playfulness, Tama-chan said, "Maybe it's funny coming from me, but I thought, *What a weird girl.*"

"Ah-ha-ha…that's what you were thinking?"

"Yep. But now…I think it's cute that you're like that."

"Ohh… Thanks." Hinami smiled, and then her gaze fixed on the food lined up in front of her. Her expression was gentle, as if she was thinking back on something, and it didn't at all look like acting.

Eventually, she smiled like she didn't know what else to do, and in a more sorrowful voice than usual, she said, "...What do I do? It feels like a waste to eat it."

"I understand the feeling! But feel free to just go for it!" said Mimimi.

We watched in silence as the three of them expressed their feelings to one another.

Hinami and Mimimi had known each other from their club in middle school. Hinami had met Tama-chan in their first year of high school, but she's also told me that Tama-chan resembles her lost sister.

I don't mean to make comparisons as to whose bond was stronger or who she'd known longer.

But I'm sure the relationship between the three of them is irreplaceable.

"Wow...this is good! Actually, this is pretty close to the real thing..."

A smile grew on Hinami's face as she tried out the salad. Once she put some in her mouth, she didn't stop, and in a blink, she'd eaten up half of the salad.

"Ah-ha-ha. I thought eating it was a waste, Aoi," Mimimi said.

"It tastes so good! I can't help it."

While watching the two of them banter back and forth, the rest of us glanced at one another and got started on the food lined up on the table.

"Ohh...this was reproduced pretty well."

Eating the salad, I was surprised, too. Of course, it wasn't a perfect reproduction. But I think it was pretty impressive to make from scratch. At the very least, there had to have been some trial and error.

"Right?! We went to the restaurant a bunch of times and had them teach us stuff!"

The other food we ate was all high quality, too, and though I couldn't share in those memories, I could tell there was special meaning in the food from Hinami's smile as she ate.

I learned that over these past few weeks, Mimimi and Tama-chan had gone to all these restaurants, and they got those that would help out to teach them the recipes. The two of them had worked together at Tama-chan's house to prepare the ingredients and sauces and whatnot, and then that day, they had brought it with ice packs to drop it off at the guest house with the luggage. Then the two of them had gotten back from USJ early to cook everything.

"That's amazing to go that far," I said.

"Uh-huh. Of course it is," Tama-chan answered bluntly. Then she gave Hinami a soft look. "I mean, Aoi's done a lot for me. This isn't even enough to repay her."

"Hanabi..."

And then smiling at her with only good feelings, Tama-chan said, "So...thanks again, Aoi."

"...No, thank you," she said, even as her voice gradually started to wobble at the end.

"Ahh! It's not fair for you to be the only one doing the thanking, Tama! I wanna thank her, too!" Mimimi said.

"Ah-ha-ha. I get it already."

"That's fine! It's still important to say these things out loud!" Then Mimimi got a bit shy. "I think without you, Aoi, I wouldn't be doing track, and my grades would be a lot worse... You've been supporting everything I do, in a way."

"Come on...that's exaggerating."

"It's not exaggerating! It's totally for real!"

As shy as you'd expect, Mimimi said, "So thanks! I respect you more than anyone in the world!" Face red, she averted her eyes a little.

It was completely different from how Tama-chan had communicated it, but I'm sure both of them were being utterly sincere.

So even the perfect heroine Aoi Hinami could barely find the words. "Yeah...thanks."

But their surprise did not end here.

After we'd more or less finished eating the food, Mimimi went to the kitchen. "And now, this is the main event for today!" she said, bringing out a luxurious and magnificent cheesecake about the size of her face.

It was topped with berries and other fruits and filled with love, along with the desire to give those who ate it joy. It didn't just look like it tasted good—it was aesthetically pleasing. It was that kind of cheesecake.

I watched to see how things would go, wondering if this also called back to some memory, but Hinami was staring blankly at the cake.

"Whoa there, Aoi! I'm guessing you don't know about this cake!"

"Huh? Y-yeah." Aoi nodded.

Tama-chan seemed almost shy. "Um…" Then she accepted the cake from Mimimi and slowly carried it over. "I told you that I wanted to get serious about helping at my family's bakery, right?"

That was enough for everyone there to get it.

Tama-chan carefully placed the dish on the table and brought it up to Hinami.

And then she set atop it a chocolate disk that read, *"Happy Birthday! Thanks for Everything, Aoi"*—and then she smiled at Hinami.

"This is the first original cake I've ever made."

Hinami was surprised, but that eventually turned to a smile. "Geez… you two are not playing fair."

"Ah-ha-ha. I still got help from my mom and dad, though."

"…But still."

While talking, Tama-chan put a knife in the cake, and she served up one slice of cake on a plate, which she gently set in front of Hinami.

Hinami took in the colorful, glistening cheesecake.

"C'mon! Eat, eat!" Minami urged her.

"But…"

"Once you've had one bite, you won't be able to stop anyway."

"Huhhh, wasn't expecting something like that from you."

Mimimi and Hinami were bantering, matching each other beat for beat as always.

I think, in a way, you could call that a formality—but that was fine, I thought.

Hinami slowly brought a forkful of the cake to her mouth. "...It's good," she murmured, and I could hear the gratitude in her voice.

Since this was Hinami, I didn't know how much of her performance I could believe.

But this was a precious moment for the nine of us.

We all followed in Hinami's lead, cut up the cheesecake, and started eating.

"Ohh! This is good!" Mizusawa said in surprise.

"...Wow, the sweetness of the berries and the smooth flavor of the cheese..." It was so good, I got rather verbose—my otaku flaw.

"I'm so glad I got the chance to eat Tama's cake...!" Whatever Takei was feeling moved about, he was half in tears as he ate.

"Ah-ha-ha...this may be your first cake, but you could sell this," Hinami said with a smile.

But Tama-chan shook her head no, also smiling. "Um, for our price range, it would be selling for less than the cost, so I can't."

"...Oh, I see. Thanks, Hanabi."

"You're welcome." As Tama-chan kindly nodded, she was smaller than any of us, but bigger than any of us.

Listening to their conversation from the side, Mizusawa and I shared a look.

"Okay, let's go, Fumiya, Fuka-chan," he said.

"Y-yeah."

"Y-yes!"

And then Mizusawa, Kikuchi-san, and I came forward.

"A-all right, guys!" I said with a little hesitation.

"Okay, then could you look at our present?" Mizusawa said, as smoothly as always.

Kikuchi-san repeated just the "C-could you?" part as we lined up in front of the projector.

If the feelings Hinami had just let show were the real thing, then I wanted her to hold on to that feeling as she saw this.

I got right to it and connected a tablet, which had a controller attached to it via USB hub, to the projector. And then I made a certain logo screen display over the whole wall.

"Throw Throw Found"

Though it was simple, since the graphics were straight out of *Atafami*, it was a pretty nice-looking opening image. It was an original that reproduced the game Hinami loved, *Go Go Oinko*, with Found from *Atafami*.

"Ah-ha-ha, what is this? A parody video?" Hinami said, laughing.

I placed the controller in front of her. "Ha-ha-ha. Nope. —It's a parody game."

"A game?" Hinami was surprised.

I watched her out of the corner of my eye as I navigated the opening screen, which displayed "story mode" and "versus mode," and went with the latter.

"See, you can actually move it."

"What the heck?! You actually made this? From scratch?"

"Yeah. I got Kikuchi-san and Mizusawa, and Ashigaru-san to help… and we got a guy to make it," I said.

Hinami giggled again. "You were just saying Tama-chan went really far. But you totally can't talk."

She was completely right.

But my answer for her was the same as before.

"Of course," I said boldly and with pride.

"You've done so many important things for me—so much that I couldn't ever repay you."

*   *   *

"...I see," Hinami said, jerking her head away in her contrarian way, but with the hint of a smile. Then she took up the controller in front of her and started playing *Throw Throw Found*.

"Huh...?" Hinami made a surprised sound.

"Ha-ha-ha, how d'you like that? Great, right?"

"These controls...," Hinami said, and I nodded with pride.

At first, Hinami had probably thought that it was just a shooter with *Atafami* characters. But this game didn't just focus on the superficial aspects of graphics and whatnot. It had been made with a focus on the gameplay—the rules and controls.

So even if it looked different, it should feel just about the same as when she had played with her sisters way back when.

"Let's play. It's been a while—," I said.

I took hold of the controller again.

"—since we've had a mirror match between two Founds."

Hinami looked exasperated, but I could tell she was looking forward to it as she smiled. "Bring it on... But..." Her expression gradually turned competitive.

It was a lot like the one she'd always get before playing *Atafami* with me. *This determined smile suits her best, after all*, I thought.

"...I have a way longer history playing this Found—are you okay with that?"

I couldn't really tell if that came from her real feelings, her mask, or what.

I think that moment, when *Oinko* and *Atafami* were mixed into one—

*　*　*

—was the very moment that a young Hinami and NO NAME blurred into one.

＊　＊　＊

"Hey, hold on! You're way too good at this, Aoi!"

"Eh-heh-heh! Hexactly. I won again."

We were all playing repeated matches of *Throw Throw Found* together. We'd been playing it under the rule that whoever loses switches with the next person, and currently, Hinami had been playing continuously without a single loss.

"But that was a pretty good game! GG, Nakamoo!"

"Shit, I was so close… The moment your HP got low, you got so damn tough." Nakamura was incredibly frustrated, having lost to Hinami by just a hair. In the most recent game, Nakamura had really taken the lead at the beginning and had gotten pretty close, but in the end, Hinami's ultra-cautious playstyle had just barely won out.

Hey, playing like that against a beginner isn't very mature, is it, Hinami?

"Does that make it…fifteen wins in a row?" Kikuchi-san said, watching Hinami with horror.

"Yeah…but…," I said confidently. "I've basically got it. I'll be okay next round."

"Ohh! I'm looking forward to it."

And so I took the controller from Nakamura for my fourth match against Hinami.

"Time to wreck you again," she said.

"Nah, this time I'm going to win."

Our gamer trash talk got the audience worked up. *Hmm, as someone aiming to be a pro gamer, I guess it really is important to offer people a show.*

And then the game began.

To play, you moved the character up and down and pressed a button to make Found throw shuriken. If that hit the other person, they'd take damage, and you'd score a certain number of points—it was a very simple system. Thanks to that simplicity, the important thing was precision of control, and Hinami had played this game for years, so her control was naturally refined, leading to this string of wins.

But I hadn't declared that I was going to win for no reason.

The key points in this game were the unique feel of the controls—the motion of the character going up and down started slow, but if you continued moving in the same direction, it accelerated—and each player could fire just two powerful projectiles. Basically, like bombs in shooters. In *Oinko*, they were bombs, but in *Throw Throw Found*, they were called flash-bangs.

The flash-bangs were powerful, and one hit would take almost exactly half of your health away, so they could turn around a match in one hit. Nakamura had managed to almost eke out a win once because Hinami had gone the wrong way early in the game and hit one of those flash-bangs.

Essentially, it was an opening in the rules. If I was to beat her, then it had to be with that.

"…"

I closely watched how Hinami moved, waiting for my opportunity.

The way Nakamura had been playing when his flash-bang had hit her had given me a hint.

The flash-bang would do massive damage—half your max HP.

Hinami was an experienced player, and it probably was no coincidence that she had touched the flash-bang.

That realization had opened up a path to victory.

"—Right here!"

The moment Hinami's Found, the one on the left side, went up to the top of the screen, I threw two flash-bangs at once with just a slight delay between them; I aimed them right under the top, where the explosion would just barely reach the top left.

"…!" Hinami panicked and changed direction, but she was too late. Since in this game, up-down movement started off slow, my shuriken hit her Found as he was trying to move downward, and then—

—Found had lost momentum and was in his stunned animation from the hit, so he was unable to avoid the other flash-bang that came for him during his invincibility frames. A second hit.

"Ahhhhh!" Hinami cried out loud. Getting hit with two flash-bangs meant Hinami's Found's HP was now zero.

"All right!"

I pumped a fist, and everyone watching cheered, too. Hinami had been winning the whole time, so her first loss got everyone excited. She was like the away team, even though it was her birthday.

"Hold on, that double bomb! That play was against the rules in the Hinami household!"

"Huh? What's that supposed to mean?" I asked.

"You always win if you time it right. We decided that strategy made it boring, so double bombing was against the rules!"

"Oh, really? …But that's too bad."

"What?"

And then I used idiot logic to tackle this matter of dispute, childishly puffing out my chest. "This isn't *Go Go Oinko*; it's *Throw Throw Found*, so that rule hasn't been made yet."

"Ngh…b-but!"

I cut Hinami off and waved a finger at her. "Tsk-tsk-tsk. Besides, you said *double bomb*, right? Unfortunately, what I used was…a double flash-bang."

Hinami gave me a frustrated glare. "Nghh. O-one more time," she said. She was such a sore loser, so childlike—or maybe gamer-like.

It made me think that we were really alike in this way.

"Okay, you two, don't get so worked up." Izumi plonked a light chop down on each of our heads. "It's about time for the games to end…and there is our surprise at the end, too, you know!"

"O-oh yeah, sorry," I apologized. "…Well, we've got all night, and we can play games any time."

"You still want to play?! There's tomorrow, too, so you need to go to bed, okay?!"

Izumi launched a mom-elemental attack and disconnected the tablet. Now displayed on the projector instead was the default screen of a DVD player.

"…A video?" Hinami said, puzzled, and Nakamura and Takei nodded with confidence.

"All right, then, finally, we have some celebratory remarks from the Association of Aoi Gratitude!" Izumi said, and then she flipped off the lights.

The projector screen was now brighter than before, and it displayed the empty hallway of Sekitomo High School.

"Aoi! Happy birthday!"

A total of six people popped out from the edges of the screen. It included Tachibana and Kashiwazaki-san, those classmates who weren't with us.

"Man, the one problem here is that we can't be there to celebrate with you when it's your big day."

"Yeah, totally! Last year was a weekday, right? We all celebrated it together."

"Once you come back, let's have a big party!"

"…Ah-ha-ha, sorry," Hinami muttered while watching that video.

In the dark, where this projector was the only light, I couldn't properly read her expression.

"You never show your weaknesses, but you're allowed to show them sometimes!"

"Ohh! Well said!"

"I-it is, isn't it?!"

"Then have a wonderful seventeenth!"

That wrapped up the remarks from everyone, and then the video ended with a clicking sound.

And so the surprise from Izumi was done—or so I thought.

The screen brightened once more.

"Aoi-senpai! Happy birthday!"

"Happy birthday, Hinami."

It showed six girls in front of the track clubroom.

In other words, this time, it was a message from her teammates in her club.

"We really admire you, Hinami-senpai! It's like you're on another level, even among the senpais!"

"Come on, give us some admiration, too."

"Huh? But that's really not the right person to be admiring!"

"Hey..."

They were all just informal birthday greetings.

But it didn't feel like they'd just filmed it because Izumi had told them to. It was as if they were openly communicating what they really thought.

"We'll keep up with this club's traditions, even after you've retired!"

"We'll teach all the newbies your way of keeping the track and field neat!"

"I'll take...take care of the...shoelaces you gabe me...Hinami-senbai!"

"Hey, don't cry! This is her birthday, not graduation."

*   *   *

"Ah-ha-ha...Shima-chan..." Hinami was laughing, but you could tell there was emotion in her voice.

The people who appeared spanned all the way from her track-club advisor who had left when Hinami was in first year, and the rival she'd competed against at track nationals, to the owner of the restaurant in Omiya with delicious cheese that she often went to.

"Aoi-chan!"

"Hinami-san!"

"Hinami!"

The names they called and their congratulations vividly indicated all the things Hinami had done.

Most of that had probably just been interaction through a cold mask for the sake of social success, proving her way was right. She was using them to tamp down her own fragility.

But—

—what Hinami had been doing for her own sake had generated this much respect and goodwill.

So many people were thankful to her and wanted her to be happy, going to the trouble of sending her birthday greetings.

"Hey, Hinami."

I thought this was one answer for the way Hinami was.

"...Now you get it, right?"

I approached her as her gaze was captured by the video, I and told her what I really thought, so that only she could hear.

Up close, her eyes appeared wet—or was that just the light of the projector reflecting off her eyes in the dark?

Or had she gotten emotionally shaken up so many times in one day that their innocent goodwill was reaching beyond her mask?

She was the only one who would know the answer to that.

"...Get what?" The voice that reached my ears sounded as if it was smothering the emotions in it by force.

"Even if it is 'formalities.' Do it over and over, and it'll reach you eventually."

I recalled a guy who had recently acquired the passion to keep going.

I was thinking of a couple who'd gone through repeated trial and error to try to attain something special.

And I was gazing at the game-loving girl in front of me, who only knew how to throw herself into battle.

"Maybe you only ever thought the stuff you've done was for your proof." Both how she dealt with everyone, and my life strategy, too. "But it's helped me, all of us here, our classmates, your teammates, and even the teachers—everyone. They've all gotten something important from you."

I was sure my words were reaching where I wanted them to.

"So that's enough."

For some reason, I could really feel that was true.

"You're enough as you are, Aoi Hinami."

And then the screen went dark again, and Izumi officiated in a cheery tone, "—All right, then the next is the final message!"

After a darkness that lasted a little longer than before, the final video began.

But then—

—the controller that had still been in Aoi Hinami's hands fell to the floor with a *clatter*.

*　　*　　*

"…Huh?"

Displayed on the big protector screen were some people I'd only met once—

"—*Happy birthday, Aoi.*"

It was Aoi Hinami's mother, and her younger sister.

Afterword

It's been a long time. This is Yuki Yaku.

It's been a year since Volume 9, which went on sale right in the middle of the anime broadcast. I feel bad that I made you wait a year after that ending of all things, but well, um, I'm feeling quite keenly that the ending of this volume will also be guilty of the same crimes. I also feel like the time has passed in a flash since the excitement of the anime, but it's also like, has it still only been a year?

But now you all have Volume 10 here in your hands, which means that finally, I can deliver this news to you.

The production of a new *Bottom-Tier Character Tomozaki* anime has been decided!

You may be wondering—what is this new anime? What exactly does that mean? I still can't say. What I can tell you is not to worry, and please look forward to it. The series has grown thanks to your support, and Omiya is the new capital. Think of it as that kind of content. I'd be glad if you could continue to support it.

Now then, speaking of the anime, I'm reminded of something that happened. I think you all know about how during the *Bottom-Tier Character Tomozaki* broadcast, Fly-san would post illustrations on Twitter during the show every week. Well, when the first episode was airing, me, my editor, Iwaasa-san; and Fly-san were having an anime watch party in real time.

It was like a festival, and we had a very fun time, but Fly-san sneakily posted a commemorative illustration right in front of us without saying anything.

I noticed when Iwaasa-san was like, "Fly-san...!" I really remember finding it, too, and getting worked up about it as Fly-san was right there in front of me, calmly smiling.

I was very moved by the cool and characteristic way Fly-san does things, Hinami's bright smile on the post, and Fly-san's thoughtfulness.

That is surely something I can't give enough thanks for—that's why this time, there's something I really must tell you all about.

That is the "clothing narrative" of the illustration on the frontispiece of this book.

I suspect people will start saying things like *Don't start with the emotional story*, *Don't put things off just because there's space in the afterword*, and *Apologize to Fly-san*, but this is the afterword, so please let me do what I want. And I will apologize to Fly-san.

Now then, about the USJ color image in this book, the truth is when I requested it, I said that it was "in front of the big globe at USJ, with the boys in regular clothing and the girls in their uniforms taking a photo," but the truth is, I left the details to Fly-san.

For example, there's how Mimimi and Tama-chan are wearing the same hats, or that only Hinami is wearing the protagonist's hat. And Kikuchi-san, who seems like she would stick out in a scene like this where others are matching, is wearing the same headband as Yuzu. And with the boys, who are wearing their regular clothes, only Takei is in his school uniform.

Those sorts of things originated with Fly-san, not me or Iwaasa-san.

And of course, if you have those ideas, that creates a story.

For example, Kikuchi-san wearing the same headband as Yuzu might be because Yuzu was worried that Kikuchi-san would stick out from the others, and so she bought her the same one.

Takei might have heard about the girls decision to do USJ-niforms. Or maybe he told all the guys, "Let's go in our uniforms!" but then he was ignored.

From the moment in the time of the illustration, it expresses that the past, the future, this world exists. That's exactly what gives Fly-san's art such depth.

It communicates with just a bit of clothing or change of facial expression the unfolding story behind the picture.

In other words—you show the interior story with only illustrations and a few words.

That is one of the many charms of Fly-san's illustrations, and it's also one of the endless list of reasons that I continue to be Fly-san's fan.

Now then, what I would like you to remember is the story that I spoke about at the beginning, about our watch party for the first episode of the anime.

Despite how Fly-san was properly preparing an illustration, we didn't say anything. We were just sneakily retweeting that illustration right in front of one another.

"You show the interior story with only illustrations and use few words."

This is what makes Fly-san's illustrations so wonderful, and it also expresses Fly-san's modesty as an illustrator. I think I could say something like that just from the illustrations and that event that happened in my life.

I would be happy if I could communicate even just some of these feelings.

Well then, the acknowledgments.

The illustrator, Fly-san: I was asked to do the afterword in a doujinshi that was distributed at Comiket, and I wound up sending in two such dubious documents in a short period of time. I've been worried sick thinking I might be sued. In the case of a private settlement, please go easy on me. I'm a fan.

To my editor, Iwaasa-san: It's become too much of a custom for me to spend the end of the year cooped up at Shogakukan. I've come to wonder if Shogakukan is a shrine. I will come to worship again soon.

And to all my readers: Just when you think the anime broadcast has ended, a new anime is announced. I think that we'll be seeing plenty more fun things, so I would be glad if you would continue to push onward with me. Thank you very much for your continued support.

Well then, I would be glad if you would join me for the next book as well.

Yuki Yaku